FOR ALL THOSE WHO PUSH THE BOUNDARIES OF IMAGINATION.

TABLE OF CONTENTS

INFESTATION
BY DEANNA YOUNG

Ciena sealed her helmet in place and opened the Hespres II's space station hatch. She triple checked the tether line, clipped her equipment to her suit, took a deep breath, and stepped out into the black abyss of space.

Getting rid of a ship's Rogue Autonomous Trasher problem wasn't hard, not anymore, but the hull inspection made her stomach tie in knots every time.

Ciena pressed the controls that steered her suit, gliding toward the docked ship. The O_2 regulator sputtered, and her heart skipped. It wasn't responding to the controls. Sweat beads formed on her forehead as she floated farther and farther away from her target. She pressed the button over and over again before it

1

connected and the propulsion system engaged, thrusting her forward. She let out a shaky breath. She'd almost died in space once before, floating alone in a malfunctioning evacuation pod. Even with the security tether she never felt safe outside of the station. *It's good. We're good.*

Once she reached the side of the ship, Ciena hooked her belt clip into the guide rail that ran along its length. She then unhooked the large box attached to her pack and secured it to the rail beside her. Both the box and the slender, silver cylinder attached to it were her creations. She pushed a button activating her Siren's Pipe, and opened the slot in the side of her modified Faraday trap. The pipe called out to the RATs, sending subsonic signals that mimicked impacts against ships and distress beacons on a low power signal to attract RATs in the immediate area.

The engineering involved in making the Trashers fascinated her. Originally designed to salvage old ships and tear down space junk, they were sturdy, nimble and efficient. Not necessarily a good quality when they went rogue, but it was a manageable problem. And it gave her a job.

Any second now. Yep. Here they come. She smiled in satisfaction as several squat little robots with metallic legs made their way toward her. The RATs looked more like crabs than rodents, but the acronym did fit with their infestation-like qualities.

One of the RATs floated toward the trap, carrying a metal scrap in a clawed hand, reluctant to abandon its find as it was pulled in by the siren's song. She opened a slot on the top of her trap and shoved the RATs inside as they reached her. One RAT swept down from behind Ciena, making her rock back in surprise as it landed on the trap. She pushed it inside with the others. Within minutes all the RATs on the hull had been collected. She closed the slot door and activated a specialized EMP, frying the main fuses.

Ciena finished up by inspecting the ship and entering repair requests on the displayed holographic schematics. She noticed the time display reflected on the inside of her helmet and gasped. It was nearly noon, she had to hurry or she'd be late for her chat with Abby.

The tether retracted, pulling her into the city-sized space station. She huffed at the slow, steady pace. There was nothing to be done about the speed, so she tried to relax and enjoy the view. This was something people traveled out of their way to see and she got to look out on it every day.

Tulorian was alive with violent storms, seemingly eager to perform for her. Deep purple clouds swirled and tumbled over each other, while blue lightning intermittently lit the planet's violet surface. This mesmerizing display was one extra incentive for travelers to stay a little longer at the Resort Station. As the view diminished behind the looming station, Ciena glanced at the clock again. She still had time, but not much.

The hatch opened, pulling her in. As it closed behind her, the heavy artificial gravity locked her to the ground, momentarily jarring her senses. She shook it off, then shed her suit, hung it on a hook, picked up her RAT trap and started for the door. She could collect payment later.

A tall, thin man called out as he chased after her. "Miss! Are you done then? Can I get my writ of decontamination? I need to get on with my repairs."

She stopped, and let out an exasperated sigh before composing herself and turning around, "Yes, of course." She waved the man forward. "I'll need payment before I sign the forms."

He dropped several blue spherical glass chips into Ciena's open palm. The small marble-like currency stuck together in a clump in her hand. Ciena raised an eyebrow at him and cleared her throat.

"We agreed on fifty."

"Yes, but I don't owe you for a full day of work, when you did the job in just a few hours."

Ciena mimicked his condescending tone, "Yes, but you would have paid twice as much if I had taken the standard two days. And you'd be waiting another day to start your repairs."

It had taken Ciena quite a while to get used to bargaining this way. No one ever wanted to pay her what her services were worth. Part of it was typical haggling, and part of it was that she was a nineteen-year-old girl, and looked like an easy mark. Ciena had spent nearly a year modifying her trap and building her pipe to make the job more efficient. But that didn't stop people from trying to convince her that she was ripping them off.

She kept her palm open, waiting. "You knew the price before I started."

The muscles in the waifish man's jaw tightened and he begrudgingly dropped one more chip in her still open hand. This chip was clear and the encased metallic bar in the center glinted as it tumbled against the other spheres and clicked into place at the bottom of the pile. It was worth ten more than the others, bringing the total up to fifty.

"Most generous. Thank you, chief," she said, pocketing the clicks and giving him a mock salute with two fingers. She signed the proffered tablet, grabbed her RAT trap and rushed out the bay doors.

After dropping the metal box and extra money off in her quarters, Ciena strode to the transport terminal weaving her way through the meandering crowd. She hopped on the tram while those around her shuffled through the open doors, staggering into comfortable positions.

The sharp smell of hydraulic fluid filled the confined space, coming from a group of machine workers standing at the front of the car. Ciena dropped her cheek to her shoulder and discreetly sniffed the collar of her own jacket then relaxed against the wall behind her. Thank goodness those space suits were well ventilated.

They rode in consensual silence as passengers checked and stowed various devices from their pockets. Ciena shifted her weight from foot to foot, suppressing a sigh as the tram stopped to let more people on.

After getting a few strange looks, she realized she was still sporting her messy mane of helmet hair and fished a handful of ribbons out of her pocket. Her fingers eventually tamed the beast, weaving ribbons through the braids as she went.

Eventually the tram came to its final stop, spilling passengers out into the station's enormous Common room. She pushed past the newcomers as they gawked at Tulorian and the ongoing storm visible through the massive viewing windows, and picked her way through the crowds of people milling in front of the various food establishments. She climbed the stairs leading up to the balcony two at a time, and walked briskly past men and women peddling services and goods from store fronts and kiosks, nodding to a few as she rushed by.

Inside the dull, sterile communications alcove of the relay station were dozens of cubicles, each with its own chair and large computer screen.

Ciena sat down at one of the terminals and took twenty-five clicks out of her pocket. The little glass spheres stuck together in a clump. She rolled them around in her palm with her thumb, pushing them apart and letting them click back together as she counted them. It wasn't much, the cost of few nice meals and a hot shower, but she always felt a little sick when she had to spend money.

A soft chime sounded as she dropped the clicks into the round slot by the screen, one by one. The screen came to life, showing twenty-five credits. She tapped the Send Chat Request button and typed 'Abby Holwick, Bitera Orphanage, Ophelia'.

While she waited for someone billions of miles away to fetch Abby, Ciena pulled a bar of Survival Sustenance out of her pocket and tried to enjoy the chewy meal. She could have bought lunch while downstairs, but she purposely didn't bring any extra clicks with her so she wouldn't be tempted. She opened up another window on the screen and checked the station logs. Her tongue dug at the pits in her teeth, trying to clear out the pieces of honeyed grain stuck there. Three ships, including a full-sized cargo ship, were scheduled to dock later today, but only two had traveled through a sector that required decontamination. Regardless, she had a busy afternoon ahead of her.

The meter in the top right corner of the screen now read '20 credits'. Ciena slouched forward in her chair, resting her elbow on her knee and propping her head on her hand. *Hurry, Abby.* She sat up, spun her chair in a circle a few times, then looked back at the computer screen and tapped the icon that said 'Book Travel'. She scrolled through alphabetic listing of destinations until she came to Ophelia. She tapped on it, and a picture of a watery planet with thousands of islands filled the screen. Two price tags lit the bottom left corner.

'Direct passage, all expenses paid, 56 days: 39,899 clicks'

'Passage via Ridel and Titan, basic accommodations, 72 days: 24,499 clicks'

Ciena opened another window and pulled up her station account. She had saved 34,743 clicks in a little over 2 years. If all went well, she could book passage for Ophelia in about a month. Hopefully the extra money she had saved would be enough to get Abby and find someplace they could call home again.

Beep, Beeeeeeep.

An incoming message interrupted her thoughts. The picture of Ophelia was replaced by the face of a seven-year-old girl with short cropped brown hair. She was wearing a tan smock and sweat was dripping down her face, making clean pink streaks in the brown dirt.

"Hi, Ciena." She said through a semi-toothless grin. The light in her eyes seemed to rekindle for just a moment, then the flame blew out.

"Hi, sweetie. How have you been?" Ciena's heart soared and ached all at once looking at her sister.

There were a few seconds of delay in the relay before she responded. "I'm good. I did get in a tiny bit of trouble for making sand castles today when I was supposed to be planting." She looked sheepish for a second, then rushed on, "Oh, and Pedra says to remind you to call *after* 6, Ophelia time. I still had fifteen minutes to plant potatoes. It takes a lot of food to feed all of us and we have to do our part..." She said the last part like a recitation.

Ciena gave an imperceptible shake of her head. Not this again. They had changed approved call times twice in the last month alone. The last time they had done so, the call time didn't correspond with relay station alignment and Ciena had to miss the call, "Okay. I'll remember to call after 6." Abby didn't need to see her upset, so she pasted on a smile and leaned toward the screen. "Guess what? I have some great news."

"What is it?" Abby asked with wide eyes.

"In about a month, I'll be heading your way. It'll still take a few months to get to Ophelia, but you can

11

start counting down now. And, I'll make a hundred sand castles with you when I get there, okay?" Abby had her hand over her mouth, letting out a tiny squeal, unable to contain it. She turned to look behind her and Ciena gasped as she noticed a large fading bruise on the back of Abby's arm.

"Abby, what happened to your arm?"

"Oh, it's nothing." She covered her arm with her other hand and rubbed it. Seeing Ciena's sharp look, she mumbled, "Just sat in the wrong spot at lunch. Some other kids didn't like it."

"Oh, Abby, I'm so sorry. Did they get in trouble?"

Abby shrugged and stared at the ground. Ciena pursed her lips but didn't press the issue further. What had happened to the bubbly little girl that bounced when she walked because she couldn't contain her happy energy? She was slowly disappearing. She'd have to write to Pedra later, not that it would do any good, but she had to try.

Ciena's eyes started to fill with tears and she blinked them back. "I'll be booking the next ship that comes through here. It's scheduled to dock here in thirty-six days." She hadn't been with Abby since that awful day, over two and a half years ago.

"Hey, you're wearing the ribbons momma gave you again. They look nice. I can't wear ribbons here." Abby said, rubbing the short cropped hair that barely touched her ears. Ciena absently touched the colored ribbons she had woven through her braids. Her mother had always loved braiding them through her hair.

"Which color do you like best?" Ciena asked. She tilted her head, touching the different colors in turn.

"Purple!" she shouted, then clapped a hand over her mouth and looked over her shoulder again. "I mean, purple is my favorite color. I love purple." she said more softly, ducking her head into her shoulders.

A hand landed on Ciena's shoulder, giving her a start. She turned and looked up at a young man with dark brown hair and a wide grin.

"Hey, Ciena. Sorry to interrupt." he said. "My father...er, I mean, Commander Hamelin wants to speak to you."

A digitalized voice from the terminal broke in, "*Deposit more currency for additional minutes.*"

"Um, just a second, Kienn," Ciena said, holding up one finger and turning around.

"Don't go yet..." Abby's face turned into an instant frown and her voice was almost too soft to hear. "I don't want to go back out to the fields today. It's almost dinner. Just talk a little bit longer. Please." She bit her lip and stared unblinkingly at Ciena through the screen.

"*Thirty seconds remaining.*" The computer announced.

"Abby, I didn't bring any more clicks. I'm sorry." She leaned in closer and brought her hand up to touch Abby's digitalized face. Tears filled the little girl's amber eyes and her bottom lip began to tremble.

The deposit chime sounded and Ciena turned to see Kienn dropping clicks into the circular slot.

He gave her a small shrug and whispered, "I'll wait for you outside." He waved to Abby before turning and walking out the door.

#

Several minutes later, Ciena walked out of the Communications Relay. Kienn jogged forward from where he had been leaning on the wall to join her. She turned away and wiped her nose with her sleeve.

"Sorry. It's just hard to see her like that. I'll pay you back later."

"Don't worry about it. Seriously."

Ciena rolled her eyes. "I *will* pay you back."

"Fine, fine." He raised his hands in mock surrender. "What was that all about, anyway? With your sister, I mean. Isn't she at the Home for Children on Ophelia?"

"Yes, if you can call it a home. They have those kids out working in the fields or workshops all day. They say that it teaches them valuable skills for the real world, but it's just free labor, that's what it is."

"I'm sorry. I didn't know it was that bad. I thought she was doing well there, that it was better for her."

"That's what everyone thought. It's not your fault. Nothing to be sorry about."

He looked down at his feet and didn't say anything while they descended the stairs. The pings and zings from the Antique Arcade faded as they left it behind. The common room was bustling with activity. Kids giggled and ran around their parents as they haggled over the prices of supplies, meals or trinkets. Men and women alike laughed as they played cards and told stories, passing the time over drinks, until their ship repairs were complete and they could hit the skies again.

A tall, thick man with crew cut hair and a bushy beard was walking up to the door in the engineering column at the center of the room. He stepped back and examined it, putting his hand on the keypad. *What was he doing?*

Kienn rushed forward, "Can I help you?"

"Oh, yes. I'm looking for the Gear Smith. I need to rent a spatial aligner." His voice was low, his accent abrasive. Ciena couldn't see his face, but his voice seemed strangely familiar. A feeling of distrust settled over her.

"His office is right next to Tram B, over that way." Kienn pointed behind the man.

He grunted his thanks and turned to head back to the offices. As he spun, his left leg went stiff and his body went rigid. "Katha!" he swore under his breath, then limped away. A chill fell from the base of Ciena's skull and scurried down her spine. The last time she'd heard that curse was the last time she ever saw her parents.

Chapter 2

Ciena stood frozen in place, staring as the man disappeared around the column. She fought the urge to follow and get a closer look at his face. This part of the galaxy was full of Katalians; hearing bits of their language wasn't completely unusual. Still, she should probably mention it to Commander Hamelin when she spoke to him. Maybe it was nothing, but maybe not. She took a deep breath, willing her mind not to think about that day.

"Ciena? Are you coming?" Kienn asked.

"Yes." She brought her gaze back to where Kienn was standing. "So, do you know why your father wanted me?" As a freelance employee, she rarely had reason to interact with the station commander.

Kienn pursed his lips into a thin line, "You know he doesn't talk to me about official business."

"So, it's official business then, huh? Did someone complain about my amazing efficiency again?"

He laughed and shook his head.

"Did someone say they found a RAT that I missed or something?"

"Maybe." He shrugged. She squinted at him, trying to tell if he was hiding something. He was never supposed to know any official business, but you could usually count on Kienn to know everything that was going on in the station, official or not. She couldn't afford any fines or suspensions right now. Not when she was so close to leaving.

"What?" He noticed her intense stare, and nudged her with his shoulder, making her canter to the side a few steps. "I actually volunteered to come get you because I wanted to invite you to play some Air Ball later. We haven't done anything together in a while..." he ran a hand through his hair, smoothing the dark waves, "My treat, of course. I need to redeem myself after that last game. I think my hover pad was damaged or something."

She raised an eyebrow at him. "Damaged? The hover pad was not damaged. Not sure about its rider, though." She punched him softly in the shoulder, glad to have something to take her mind off of Abby and the Commander.

He crossed his arms and turned to face her as they stopped in front of the office doors, "You only beat me by five points and that hover pad *was* acting up."

"Well, I'd be happy to give you a rematch then. It'll probably be after nine though. It's a busy day."

"That's perfect. I have to leave for a water mining run in just a bit. We won't be back until close to nine anyway."

"Didn't you guys go just last week?" She tried to keep her voice casual. When Kienn was gone, the station felt so empty.

"Yeah, but we've had several cargo fleets this week that needed their tanks refilled, so we're running low again." He shrugged and smiled in a, *this is just station life*, kind of way, then inclined his head toward the door, "Well, good luck. I'll see you after nine. And no messing with my hover pad if you get there first." He wagged a warning finger at her as he walked backward, then turned and jogged off to the tram terminals.

"I've never done that!" she yelled after him.

Once his figure faded into the crowd, she turned back around to face the office doors. She took a deep breath and pushed the entry button on the panel. The doors opened with a low hiss and Commander Hamelin looked up from where he was standing, leaning on his desk. His thick eyebrows and short brown beard with flecks of grey made him look especially intimidating. He looked up and waved her in with a smile. Some of the tension melted away as she thought about how his family had taken her in and helped her adjust until she got on her feet.

"You wanted to see me, sir?" Ciena stepped inside and the doors shushed closed.

"Have a seat, please." He gestured to one of the chairs and sat down in his own.

Ciena's mind started to race again. She thought about every interaction she had had with guests over the last week or two, every job she had done and every conversation with station employees as she took the short walk across the room to the chair. What could this be about?

Commander Hamelin lifted a tablet and turned it to face her. "So, I see you're leaving us. I got your application to end your station contract a few days ago."

She relaxed in her seat. So this was why he'd called her in. "Yes, sir. I turned my papers in a little early because I wanted to give you time to find someone to apprentice under me before I left."

"I do appreciate that. And I've already found someone. He's on his way from Lutus and will be here within a couple of weeks." He cleared his throat and sat back in his chair. "There is another matter to discuss." He tapped the tablet a few times.

"I called you in here today so that we could begin the process of settling your accounts." She folded her arms, gripping her elbows.

"You owe the station about fifteen thousand clicks from your hospital stay and other fees associated with the expense of outfitting your business, along with your station tax." The color drained from Ciena's face. Fifteen thousand clicks. It would take almost a year to save up that much. Abby's disappointed face flashed in her mind.

"Sir...this can't be right. I was told by the head nurse herself that I didn't need to worry about my stay in the hospital once I began working here. Every supply I've ever used or piece of equipment I've borrowed was for work on the station or for its guests." She glared at him, daring him to contradict her.

"That's all true if you are a station employee. You are not. You are a free-lance contractor. If, after five years, you had still been working with us and in good standing with the station, those fines would be absorbed and you would no longer owe them. She misspoke." He looked chagrined. "I'm sorry, you weren't informed properly."

"Are you kidding me?" Ciena spat. "I've worked hard here. I pay my rent on time and my contractor tax without complaint. I don't even know what this *station tax* is. She was standing now, looking down at the commander. "I can't stay here for another year! I need to get to Abby. You remember her? My little sister, the one YOU sent to live in an orphanage while I was unconscious in your hospital wing. You sent her away, without my permission, without anyone's permission, and I've been trying to get back to her ever since!"

Commander Hamelin pursed his lips and held up his hand to stop her rant. "Ciena, enough. First of all, ignorance of certain protocols is not reason enough to invalidate them. We can't have people coming to our station, feeding on our hospitality and skipping out the first chance they get. It's not a sustainable business model. Second of all, I sent your sister away to a place that is meant for children. She had no family--"

"She had me!" Ciena yelled, interrupting him.

"Yes, and we didn't expect you to actually survive." The commander paused, looking awkward. He hadn't meant to tell her that. "I'm sorry, but it's true. It may not have been the best decision, but we did what we thought was right at the time. Ships heading that way don't come by very often. If we didn't send her then, she may have been waiting for six months or more."

"Every piece of material I have ever used has gone to benefit the station." She pulled the Siren's Pipe out of her pocket and held it up. "This pipe is my invention. Mine. Without it, you wouldn't be getting nearly as many ships passing through this station as you do, and you know it! There is no reason for you to charge me more."

Commander Hamelin put up his hands, "Ciena, calm down. There's something else I need to discuss with you." His fatherly tone made her even more angry.

Ciena backed away, knocking the chair over. How could he do this to her?

She was being held hostage. They needed her.

She narrowed her eyes and gritted her teeth, glaring at the Commander. "*Sir*, I have a schedule to keep." She gave him a curt nod, then spun on her heel and stalked out of the room.

Commander Hamelin called after her, "Ciena, wait. I wasn't finished. I wanted to talk to you about your pipe—"

My pipe?

An urgent, mumbled voice over his intercom interrupted him and he didn't follow after her.

Chapter 3

People bustled about the shuttle bay, loading items into the open cargo doors of the mining ship. Along one wall of the room, two men and a woman were chatting as they buttoned up their suits and fastened gear into place.

Ciena marched up to Kienn and pushed him.

Kienn's feet shuffled and he rolled against the wall, trying to keep his balance.

"You knew! You knew what was going on. Did you help plan it too? You're supposed to be my friend!" All activity in the bay stopped. Everyone was staring at them.

"What's going on?" Kienn looked around at the spectators, "Look, we can talk about this later. I swear, I didn't--"

"You don't need to explain. It's perfectly clear that you and your father are just holding me hostage. No one else matters. Not me, and certainly not a little 7-year-old girl who's been isolated from the only family she has left for over two years while slowly working herself to death in a labor camp masquerading as an orphanage!" Hot tears spilled over the edges of her wide, maddened eyes.

He grabbed her elbow and led her away from the others. His expression was pained, "Look. I really have to go. I think you're misunderstanding something. I'll talk to you about it tonight."

"No. There's nothing to talk about." She pulled her arm out of his grip.

"Kienn." A middle-aged woman called out to him from the open loading platform on the shuttle. "We need to leave."

"I'll find you when I get back." He said, shaking his head as he turned and headed for the shuttle.

Ciena ran in the opposite direction, out the doors and down the corridor, drawing stares as she passed. She had to get away. Her vision was too blurred to see the faces of those she passed, and she was glad for that. Her lungs felt like they were filled with stones, grating against each other and weighing her down. After several minutes, she stopped running. Her shoulders ached and her head hurt.

Ciena wrapped her arms around her stomach trying to lessen the feeling of nausea that was working its way into her chest. Had she been too harsh with Kienn? No. No, this *was* a big deal. For over a year she had been meticulously counting every click, calculating how much money it would take to get to Abby, move them both to a new planet, and find a place to call home. Now, she had to break the news to her sister that it was going to take months longer than planned to get to her.

The com-link clipped to her belt buzzed, alerting her that the ship scheduled to dock this afternoon was on its way to the designated bay. She closed her eyes, trying to calm herself. *Suck it up, buttercup. If you want to ever get off of this floating hotel, you've got to get to work.*

#

Ciena looked down at the box. It was over half full, but she was already running behind by nearly an hour. She didn't want to take the time to dismantle the

RATs and empty it out. There would be plenty of time for that later, since she no longer had any plans. She frowned, feeling the anger start to rise.

Her father would have never stood for this ridiculous five-year protocol. Then again, he wouldn't have taken so long to rescue Abby. Two and half years and she still couldn't get to her. She was failing him and her mother; failing them all.

Before she realized it, she was standing in front of the open cargo door to a large freighter ship. The crew had been allowed to disembark earlier in the day, but the ship itself had only been allowed to dock for decontamination an hour earlier.

Grateful for the already open door, Ciena headed in and set to work. She plugged her pipe into the slot on the side of the Faraday trap and flipped the switch on. An erratically blinking green light on the side indicated it was sending out the subtle pulses and signals that called the RATs in.

Within minutes, several RATs were scurrying out of the ship towards her. She opened up the slot on top of her Faraday Trap and picked up the RATs one by one, tossing them in. Once they were all in, she hit the EMP button and shut them down.

The next step always took the longest and Ciena hated the cramped spaces, but for once, she actually welcomed the quiet seclusion of the maintenance tubes. She opened up a large side panel on the ship and pushed the trap through the opening in front of her, then climbed in herself.

She lifted and fit the panel door in place behind her, then pulled out her pipe to begin scanning for RATs. As she tuned the dial, she heard footfalls on the bay floor coming toward the ship. She should let them know she was here. She turned the handle on the panel, but before she pushed it open a familiar voice made her stop dead. Her hair stood on end. She knew one of those voices. She would never forget it.

"...you sure they're down? No chance for outgoing communications at all?" The voice was low and faintly accented. A chill crept up Ciena's spine. It was definitely him. It was Captain Lars.

Shouts erupted in her mind. Her father fighting a man. Yelling to get to the pods. A chair smashing down again and again on his attacker. Katha. Katha. Katha. That horrid curse. The flash of light. A body on the floor. Her mother's screams, then silence as the pod launched.

Ciena's chest and throat ached, as she forced the memories back. Those men, those pirates, were now on this space station. Her hands went to her mouth and she breathed hard into them, trying to keep from crying

"Yes, sir. Cye finished reprogramming them over a quarter hour ago. They have no idea outgoing messages are blocked." His accent was so thick, it was hard to make out what he was saying.

The limping man that had cursed in the common room earlier, he had been on the crew. *I never interacted with him though, I couldn't be sure. I still should have said something. How could I have forgotten? Stupid, stupid, stupid.*

"Our men are in position as well?"

"Just waiting on your order, sir."

Ciena wrapped her arms around her knees to keep herself from shaking, and the panel handle clicked softly as it settled itself into place.

"What was that?"

"What was what?"

Ciena froze, afraid to move, afraid to blink.

"Nevermind. I just thought I heard something."

She held her breath, sure they could hear her heart beat as it thrummed loudly in her ears.

"Don't get all jumpy on me now. It's just the ship settling." Captain Lars said, scolding the other man, "Let's do this before someone gets *wise*." He growled the last word as if that would be a real irritation to deal with.

There was the familiar scratchy static blip of a com link being pressed down, and then the second man said, "It's a go. Take out the commander, now. Let's move."

Chapter 4

The station's sirens blared to life. The attack had started. Could the station guards stop them? What type of protocols would the station follow? Would she end up as collateral damage as they opened fire on the retreating ship? Hundreds of questions raced through Ciena's head.

She shuffled backward, careful to make as little noise as possible. There was a vent a few feet back that would have a view of what was going on. Maybe she could sneak out while no one was watching. She pushed a vent blade, making it tilt open. Three men were guarding the ship. They had guns trained on the door that exited the docking bay. No, sneaking out was not an option. Maybe a distraction? Her mind raced trying to think of something she could do to draw the guards away. Could she get to the controls of the ship and cause a malfunction that disabled it?

Too late. Shouts and the sound of large objects being heaved on board and dropped could barely be heard over the noise of the sirens.

Subtle vibrations moved through the tube accompanied by a barely audible thrum. The ships engines had turned on. They were preparing to disembark.

The guards moved to the rear of a group of pirates wearing gas masks of some kind, guarding their flank. All of the pirates exiting the station were wearing gas masks. Two of them were carrying a large cube with pulsing blue lights. A second dark cube followed along behind the first. Ciena's heart skipped a beat.

That was the power transformer and energy modulator that helped the station regulate and redistribute the power it captured from the distant sun and occasional flares. Without it, the station would run out of power in its backup cells within a few days. The pirates had the main cube and the backup. The occupants of the station would freeze to death as the environmental shield failed and temperature systems could no longer keep up with the demands of the station. *They have no idea outgoing messages are blocked.* They couldn't even call for help. Contact from this far out wasn't regular and any radio silence that lasted less than a day was usually discounted as solar interference of some kind.

The lack of exchanged fighting and the steady, but not rushed manner of the pirates made Ciena's blood run cold. Was everyone already dead? *No, don't think like that.*

Ciena set her jaw. *I will not watch this happen and do nothing. Not again.* Thinking furiously, she counted the few assets she had. Her pipe, her trap, the RATs in the trap, items left in the maintenance tubes, access to a limited number of ship systems and her brain. What if she used the RATs to disable the ship, then grabbed the energy modulator cubes and escaped inside an evacuation pod? Then, it would give other travelers a chance to come to the station, find out what had happened and search for the pirates. They would find her, right? Maybe. It was a plan. A stupid, suicidal plan, but at least it was something.

#

The ship shuddered and the bay doors slammed closed with an ominous clunk. The loading area was crowded with crates, bags and armloads of goods that had been looted from the station. Men removed facemasks, clapped each other on the back and laughed.

"Hold off on your celebrations. We're not out of the woods yet, boys. We've got to make it through the sling before we're home safe." said the bearded man who she had seen earlier near engineering. He limped away following Captain Lars to the prow of the ship and waved for the others to follow.

Using the sling was the only reason she could figure that they would have blocked outgoing communications, so that made sense. If the station was able to get word out about their attack, all of the Hyper Jump Slings would be frozen until the Galactic Federation released them.

It would be a little over thirty minutes before the band of pirates made it to the hyper jump point. Ciena pulled the cylindrical pipe out of her pocket. She stared at it for a long moment, and then closed her eyes, saying a silent prayer to any God out there that may be listening. Before she opened her eyes, a picture of the full and vibrant Common room filled her mind. She could almost hear the carefree laughter from only a few hours ago. This plan of hers was their only chance, she was their only hope.

Pushing the RAT trap in front of her, she crawled along the twisted maintenance tunnels that crisscrossed around the ship like some sort of unseen cage. Eventually, she found herself underneath the engine room, looking up at a giant circuit box. She brought the pipe out of her pocket again and flipped up the top. After a second's hesitation, she popped the housing off of the tuning dials, gently pulled free some of the wires and stripped the plastic insulation off the ends. Then set to work, connecting the wires to others in the circuit box.

She turned the dials on the pipe, making calculations in her head, then tapped out a beat and held her breath. A little green light on the side of the pipe lit up and began flashing, indicating that it was transmitting the signal over all of the ships outgoing channels. Even at max output, the signal was subtle enough that it would be dismissed as static and simply filtered out if anyone decided to use the comms. Hopefully.

The pipe dangled from the circuit box, swinging lightly back and forth. Ciena reached up and unthreaded one of the ribbons from her hair. It was the purple one and the sight made her chest tighten. She tied the pipe securely to a thick wire inside the circuit box, "I'll buy you a whole slew of purple ribbons, Abby...if I somehow survive this." She murmured as she closed the door. Any RAT within one hundred hectors should be frantically making their way to the ship, following the Siren's song from her pipe.

Now for part two of the plan. She needed to get the RAT trap as far away from here as possible before she unleashed them on the ship. Ciena wrapped her jacket around the trap to muffle the noise as she pushed it so she could go a little faster than before.

She was nearly on the other side of the ship, when the heavy box caught against a raised rivet; ripping her jacket and drumming against the bottom of the box as her momentum carried it forward. The sound reverberated down the corridor.

"Hey, what was that?" a muffled voice said.

"I dunno. Sounded like it came from over here."

Ciena's chest felt like it held a couple of caged birds, fluttering and banging into each other as they tried to escape. She lifted the lid to the trap, grabbing a trapped RAT from earlier, nearly dropping the RAT in her haste. A rush of heat ran through her body as her shaking hands replaced the fried fuse and turned the mechanical beast on. She tossed it back down the corridor, and pulled the box behind her, around a bend in the tube.

"It's coming from in here. Get that panel off, Cye."

She hugged her knees and held her breath.

"Bah! It's just a stupid RAT." Several flashes of light lit up the tube. With each one, Ciena squeezed herself tighter and tried not to jump. The smell of hot metal and wisps of smoke filled the tube as a flashlight scanned the walls. "I thought that exterminator got rid of all of 'em. Wasn't this station supposed to have that prodigy kid?"

"They're bound to miss one, once in a while, Jeb. 'Sides, it ain't right to talk ill of the soon-to-be-dead." he said in a mockingly pious voice.

"Yeah, we exterminated their exterminator."

They both chuckled.

The panel made a *whump, whump* sound as it was fit back in place. Their voices faded until the only sounds were the thrum of the ship's engine and the blood pulsing in Ciena's ears.

She didn't trust herself to push the box any farther. She'd have to set the RATs loose here and hope that they were far enough away from the pipe not to reach it for a long while. She needed the signal going strong for as long as possible. One by one, she pulled the little robots out of the trap and fitted them with new fuses--grateful that the maintenance stations in the tubes had been well stocked--while at the same time adjusting some of their circuitry and programing. A normal Autonomous Trasher, even a rogue one, would spend weeks searching for components to repair itself, or salvage, before tearing apart the "junk" it came across. She bypassed that particular protocol on each of the RATs as she pulled them out, setting them into a destructive frenzy, which was doubled for these ones due to the modifications she made to the pipe signal itself. They squirmed and wriggled in her hand, eager to set to work. Multiple plier-like claws reached for objects before she even set them down. Compartments in the RATs opened up with lasers and clamps, setting to work on the pipes and frame.

The RATs soundlessly cut down and tore away pieces of pipe, wires and walls, working their way out in the direction of the hull. Ciena smirked. These were incredible machines. Incredibly terrifying. Most people didn't realize how quiet RATs actually were, or what they were capable of. Detecting them was rather difficult, and they could do a lot of damage before they were discovered, which is what made her job on the station so valuable.

Ciena crawled back toward the loading bay, leaving the RATs to their dirty work. Before she reached the other side of the ship, it slowed, causing her stomach to lurch. The gravitational dampeners must be damaged, or there wouldn't have been a noticeable change inside the ship as it decelerated.

Hopefully, that meant that the other RATs in the quadrant were responding to her signal, or maybe the RATs on the ship were doing more damage than she had anticipated. Either way, she didn't have much time to carry out the rest of her plan. Her knees were bruised from knocking against the tunnel floors, but she pushed through the pain and on to the loading bay.

Once there, she peeked through the vent. The room was empty. The guards were long gone and all was quiet. Directly in front of her were the two Energy Modulator cubes.

The panel door made a popping noise as she pushed it open. Her shoulders stiffened and her ears rang as she strained to hear any movement. After she was sure that no one had heard, she dropped to the floor. As soon as her feet touched the ground, her skin came to life, hair standing on end, seeming to sense the very air around her.

Every step she took was careful and slow. She laid a shaking hand on the cube, relieved it hadn't been dismantled for its valuable parts yet. She tried to lift it, but it barely moved. It was a lot heavier than it looked. She couldn't just tuck it under her arm and carry it off to an Evac Pod.

Looking around at the crowded room of stolen loot, Ciena saw what she needed. Leaning against one of the crates, was an Air Ball hover pad. She grabbed it and carefully pushed the Energy Modulators onto the pad, stacking one on top of the other. A musical power-up tone sounded when she turned it on, and she jumped backwards, cursing under her breath. Her heart raced madly as she pushed the energy modulator cubes towards the doorway. It was working. They glided easily along the floor.

The door loomed in front of her. It was the final barrier to freedom, but it also separated her from men who would kill her first and ask questions later. She couldn't leave the room completely unarmed. No guns, poles or any other obvious weapons lay among the stolen goods. Everything she could see was too big, too soft or too awkward to wield. There was a tool locker a few feet from her and a large heavy wrench hung inside the door on a hook. She seized it and slung it over her shoulder.

Steeling herself to run the gauntlet, she took a deep breath and punched the button to open the doors. They hissed open smoothly and she started to push the hover pad over the threshold when it powered down on its own. Now was not the time for this thing to start acting up. She muted the power-up button this time before she turned it on and shoved it out the door the second it started to float.

As soon as she stepped out to follow, an alarm sounded. The sound hit her body like a jolt of electricity and every muscle tightened in response. The urge to run and hide took hold and using the cubes on the hover pad as a shield, she started sprinting down the corridor.

A loud, harsh voice sounded over the ship's intercom system, "All men to stations. Emergency procedure delta in place."

Ciena relaxed a fraction. She hadn't activated the alarm. The ship was on alert and she hoped she knew why.

After a couple of minutes she turned a corner, and midway down the hall was a line of escape capsules with clear reinforced glass doors. She had made it. With the help of the wrench and some effort, she pried the control panel off the wall next to the first capsule she came to. She studied the box for a few seconds, found the wire she wanted and pulled it free from its fitting. Then on an impulse, pulled the wire that resealed the evacuation tubes after launch, and shoved the panel roughly back into place.

As soon as she pushed the button to eject the pod, an alert would sound and the whole ship would be notified that the Evacuation Pod had been activated. To make matters worse, it would take thirty seconds for the pod to pressurize. She didn't have any idea how to disable the ship's weapons system, so once she ejected, she'd be a sitting duck. Like her mom had been.

Tears blurred her vision for a second and her breath caught in her chest. Last time she was in an evacuation pod, a malfunction had nearly killed her. She lifted a trembling hand and pushed the button that opened the pod. Once the cubes were in, there was very little room left for her, but she squeezed in beside them and shut the door.

The cubes were wedged up against the release handle. It couldn't be pulled down and the cubes wouldn't move. She wiggled into the small space on the side of the pod and tried to move the cubes to the front, clearing them away from the release handle. As she did so, a large, broad shouldered man with beady eyes came around the corner followed by several other men. It was him. Captain Lars.

She willed herself to turn invisible, just hoping they wouldn't see her, hoping they'd keep walking. The men were climbing into their own Evacuation Pods. Captain Lars stopped in front of hers, but didn't notice her. He was trying to open the pod door, but the keypad wasn't responding. The override wouldn't work if the wires weren't connected to the keypad. Her foresight had paid off. She lifted her legs as high as she could, bracing her feet against the pod wall and pushed with her shoulders against the cubes, shoving them back, then reached up and pulled the handle.

A mechanical voice filled the pod. "Pod will be activated in thirty seconds. Thirty, twenty-nine, twenty-eight..."

The commander's head snapped up and his face went from surprised and confused, to raging anger when he spotted her with the cubes. He pounded on the door with such force that Ciena thought it would shatter at any moment. He stepped back to run at the pod and his foot caught on something. The wrench! He grinned wickedly and lifted it above his head. He brought it down on the pod, over and over again. *Thwack! Thwack! Thwack!* Ciena flinched with every strike. The commander screamed and his eyes bulged.

"...Nine, Eight, Seven, Six..." the voice continued calmly.

The wrench connected more solidly as Lars raged. *Thwack! Thwack!* He was going to break through.

With a sudden jolt, the pod exploded out of the ship and Ciena was pushed back as she hurtled away from Lars. He grabbed madly at the side of the ship, as he was sucked into the inky blackness of space. Ciena had disabled the airlock that was supposed to close off the Evacuation Pod launch tube, sealing his fate. She watched the tumbling figure grow smaller and smaller, as she was propelled farther and farther away.

She shifted her focus to the ship, and her eyes widened in shock. From this far away, the ship looked like an abandoned piece of bread at a picnic, covered in a writhing mass of ants. She didn't know there were this many RATs in the entire quadrant. How had they gotten there so fast? She started laughing. It had worked.

A few more pods ejected from the other side of the ship. The pirates had packaged themselves up neatly for the Galactic Federation to collect when they eventually came to the rescue.

Rescue. The thought of being rescued hadn't even crossed her mind since she first made her plan. She had only been worried about sabotage and escape. How long would it be before she would be rescued?

A flat mechanical voice sounded through the pod, cutting off her train of thought.

"*Pressurization failure imminent, approximately one hour to full failure. Rescue beacon has been activated.*"

Chapter 5

Ciena started to hyperventilate. Not **again**. Not another failure. Two years ago she had awoken in the hospital wing at the Space Station, cold to her bones, unable to get warm, unable to breathe on her own. What was going on in the station? Could someone come get her? Were they already dead? No, not yet. They couldn't be.

She took a few calming breaths and tried to think. It couldn't end like this. She wished she hadn't yelled at Kienn. He had been such a good friend and- and he wasn't on the station!

The cubes were annoyingly in the way as she tried to shimmy past them to reach the communications panel. She unclipped the communication device from her belt and fitted it into the port. She prayed that the signal on the pod would be strong enough to reach him.

"Kienn? Kienn, it's Ciena. Can you hear me?" There was no response. She waited a few seconds and tried again. "Kienn, it's Ciena. Please." Soft static was the only response.

She closed her eyes and felt cold tears run down her hot face. "Kienn, please. Are you there?" Nothing.

She turned and stared out of the window. Several bodies floated in the space surrounding what was left of the ship. Her stomach clenched, in spite of herself. These people were the reason her parents were gone. The reason Abby was so far away from her. The reason they never reached their new home. *Oh, Abby, I'm sorry.* She leaned against the cubes and groaned. Her head felt heavy and all she wanted to do was sleep. Was the pod failing already? She was so tired. If the station didn't get the cubes back, they would all die too. This was a disaster. Maybe Kienn would find the cubes in time, even if she didn't make it.

"I thought you didn't want to talk to me?" the voice startled her and she smacked her fist against the controls as she rushed to hit the outgoing com key.

"Kienn? Where are you?"

"We're just finishing up here with our water mining. We'll be heading back to the station in just a few. You decide you want to hear-"

"Listen, Kienn. While you were away from the station, we were attacked. The outgoing comms were knocked out."

There was a brief silence, "How are you contacting me then?"

"I'm stuck in an evacuation pod by the sling point. I...I destroyed their ship, but my pod is losing pressure. I have both of the stations energy modulation cubes too. Can you please hurry? I really don't want to spend a few weeks in the hospital again."

"Yeah, we're on our way. Just hang on, or whatever you do in those pods. Try not to break anything else."

#

Ciena sat up, feeling dizzy and nauseated. She was sitting on a bed in the hospital wing at the Space Station. This was familiar. Her body ached and it felt like her bones had been replaced with ice.

"Good to see you're awake."

Ciena turned to see Commander Hamelin a few beds down from her, hooked to several machines, shooing away a nurse who had been taking his vitals.

"Commander, I thought that you were...um, I heard the pirates say that they were going to take you out?" Ciena said.

"Yes, well. They did try. Thanks to some clever engineering on this station, and some lucky circumstances that we don't need to go into, I survived. I guess I'm tougher than they expected." He said, chuckling, and then grabbed his side with a grimace.

"Where there any casualties then?" She asked, following his gaze as he looked across the room at three tables draped with white cloths.

"Yes, three too many. Two security guards from Engineering and a guest who tried to intervene." He shook his head, "Thankfully, they miscalculated the amount of poisonous gas they needed. Instead of being lethal, it acted as a potent sedative. Maybe that's what they intended, they knew they wouldn't be leaving any witnesses on the station once the back-up batteries died."

The door to the hospital wing hissed open and Kienn stepped inside the room. He stopped mid-stride, then smiled and rushed to Ciena's side. "It's so good to see you're awake."

Ciena smiled up at him. "Yeah, it's kind of been a crazy day, huh?"

Commander Hamelin waved his hands as if clearing the air of foul smoke and changed the subject, "You're here just in time, Kienn. We both wanted to talk to you, and it really can't wait." He passed a tablet to Kienn, who handed it to her. She took it hesitantly and scrolled to the bottom where a balance of negative forty thousand clicks was highlighted.

"Just so there isn't any confusion, the station is paying *you* twenty-five thousand clicks. It's slightly more than we were offering before, as some of the docked ships chipped in to cover your medical expenses from now and from before, so those will all be cleared, and the plans for your pipe are obviously a little bit more valuable than we thought." Commander Hamelin said.

"Wait, what do you mean by *more* than before?" she asked.

"Well, apparently, father didn't get a chance to negotiate with you before. He did bring you in to settle your accounts and part of that was offering to buy your pipe from you too." Kienn said, giving her a *don't you feel foolish* grin.

"...But that wasn't...I was just, I could have swore...he didn't..." she stammered. Her face heated up and she dropped her head into her hands.

"Actually, I hadn't even managed to give you any of that information yet. You were a little worked up and I didn't have the chance to explain before you left." Commander Hamelin gave her an apologetic smile, once again adopting that fatherly persona.

Kienn cleared his throat, "We're really glad you're awake, because we also had a question for you." He looked at his father for support, who nodded at him. "Well, there's a transport ship stopping in Ophelia in a few days. It's scheduled to stop here on its way to Tritos. It's actually the same ship that is bringing my Aunt here. We were hoping you would consider bringing

Abby *here* and maybe staying on the station?" He paused and looked at her, trying to gauge her reaction. Seeing her stunned face, he rushed on, "We can book her passage today and start the paperwork with the orphanage. My aunt can act as her guardian until she arrives. You know, since she isn't twelve yet, and can't travel alone. The money you've saved can pay for her passage here, instead of your passage there. Of course, we wouldn't be buying your pipe any longer if you stayed. So, we'd have to reconfigure all of those numbers. It's up to you. No pressure."

Ciena looked up at the ceiling, shook her head and laughed as tears slid down her cheeks. This was the only family she had left. This *was* her home.

"Well, I had been looking forward to punching Pedra in the nose when I collected Abby..." Her bodied tingled and goose bumps rose on her skin, "...but, I'd love that. I think I *will* stay. *We* will stay." She said. "Oh! I've got to order some purple ribbon. Purple everything. We'll have a purple party. She'd love that, don't you think?" Ciena asked Kienn as she stepped off the table and walked around the other beds to give Commander Hamelin a gentle hug.

"Of course she would." Kienn agreed, smiling broadly as he pulled Ciena away into a tight hug of his own and kissed her on the top of the head, "Welcome home, Ciena. Welcome home."

JACK AND THE QUANTUM FRACTURE
BY BRET CARTER

I used to read to Mom every night by the light of a
candle. It was one of our last luxuries. All the candles
were marked in half-inches with a Sharpie. When the
wax wept to the next line, I would blow out the light. In
those days, darkness always had the final say.

One night, we sat at the table and I read from a
book of fairy tales. It was actually only half of a book.
Once upon a time, someone ripped it in two. My mom
had rescued it from the free-bin outside the used
bookstore in town and gave it to me for my seventeenth
birthday. I liked it a lot because it made me believe I
could maybe eventually be the missing half.

This was not long after the Quantum Fracture.
People in town told us all about it. About how

something called the Annihilation Engine was being tested just outside the atmosphere. From what I pieced together, they got the engine to work, but it busted the laws of physics or something like that.

On that particular night, I closed the half-a-book early. I had a fraction of an inch to tell her some bad news.

Mom often used the candlelight to examine the pennies she gleaned from the wishing fountain in front of city hall. No one ever stopped her and she reassured me the coins still had traces of wishes clinging to them.

She took them in to the bank to exchange them for dollars, but while she sorted through them, she took the time to look for wheat pennies—especially ones with flaws. Someone had told her those were worth a fortune.

When I set the half-a-book down, she reluctantly looked up from the penny in her palm, still squinting. "What is it, Jack?"

"We lost another cow, Mom."

She placed the penny on the table. "It's missing?"

"No, Mom. The same thing as the other two."

My mother put her hands over her face. "Oh, Jack. Really?"

Even though she couldn't see me, I nodded.

Dropping her hands, she leaned back heavily. "Are you sure it's not coyotes?"

"It's not like something with teeth, Mom. More like something with scalpels. Like they've been dissected."

She rubbed her eyes. "You're saying someone is dissecting our cows?"

I didn't have an answer so I looked at the candle. The flame had reached the next black mark.

She looked away and I blew softly on the flame.

It didn't struggle at all. It just went out.

***

In the morning, when I pulled the pillow off my face, I could see my breath. The frost had come early.

When I shuffled into the kitchen, it was empty. Mom was still in her room.

I got a carrot out of the bin for breakfast and went to the barn to tend our remaining two dozen cows. I set them out to graze, got the tool box, and spent most of the day mending the fence.

We had sold a lot of my dad's tools. All we had left was in that tool box. And the shovel. I was determined to keep that shovel. It had been my father's first tool. And if it came down to it, that shovel would be my last.

When I came home, it was late afternoon and I was pretty hungry. I was still pretty far away from the house when I smelled the fireplace going. I was surprised to see a thread of smoke coming out of the chimney. We were saving the wood for when the snow came. I couldn't figure out what she was doing.

I hurried up the steps and noticed Mom had left the shovel propped up next to the door. Lately, she had been turning some of the soil for pumpkins.

When I walked in the door, I was shocked to see that not only had she built a fire, she was actually cooking over it.

She was even smiling a little. "I've made a decision. It's time to selling everything."

Part of me was afraid to hear this. Part of me was relieved. "Really?"

"We'll start with the cows. Take just one into town and talk to Jacob."

"Jacob?"

"At the feed store."

"I know, but—"

"He told me some of the kids in the city are wanting to try their hand at 4-H. He said he could get a decent price. Dinner will be ready when you get home."

"You want me to take just one?"

"It will be faster than trying to rustle all twenty-five on foot."

"Twenty-four."

She grimaced. "Twenty-four. If he likes the one, I'm sure he'll come and get the rest."

I put on my baseball cap. In fifteen minutes, I was walking to town with one of our cows plodding along behind me tied to a rope.

The dirt road from our house didn't have a name. But it led to a gravel road called County Road 12. From there, it was another three miles to town.

No cars came along. No trucks. No tractors. No nothing.

There wasn't much to look at during the trip. Just the colorless sky over a colorless world. I watched my feet. I watched the way they just kept finding another step. Another. Another. Another.

So I didn't even see the guy until we collided. He was walking the other way and apparently, he'd been watching his feet too.

I touched my hat. "Sorry."

"Hello, there," the man said. "It's a pleasure to meet you." He wore brand-new overalls and brand-new boots. I almost expected to see the price tags dangling down.

He had gray hair and the worn-down look of someone in the suburbs of fifty, but his eyes had the shine of a toddler. "An animal," the man said.

I lifted the rope slightly. "Yep."

"Meat," the man with the toddler eyes said. And I think it was at that moment I started thinking of him as Todd. It was then or maybe later on.

Standing there with that pitiful cow tethered like a leaky leather balloon, I didn't say anything. I was trying to make sense of the conversation.

Todd's toddler eyes almost sparkled at the cow. "Meat," he said again.

The sun had melted the frost, but even so, I felt a chill along the back of my neck. I tried to veer the conversation closer to normal. "Yep, I suppose she's just a walking Happy Meal, huh?"

Todd seemed to notice the question mark in my voice only after thinking about it. His eyes twitched over to me and then back to the cow. "Happy food."

Before I could decide on a response to that bit of oddness, Todd reached into the pocket of his bright blue overalls and brought his fist out, holding a handful of something. He stepped forward and knelt down beside the cow.

At first, I thought he was going to look the animal over and make an offer.

Instead, Todd opened his right hand, palm up.

There were five pieces of metal. About the size and shape of beans. Like pinto beans. Except they were bright silver.

Todd took one of the silver beans and pushed it into the ground with his thumb, directly beneath the cow.

65

Then he selected a second silver bean and pushed that into the ground as well, a few inches from the first one.

"Wait," I said. "What are those?"

The man pointed at the first hole. "One for up and down." He pointed at the second hole. "One for side to side." Pressing the third silver bean into the ground, he said, "One for forward and backward." He planted the remaining two. "One for moments. And one for phasing."

I tried to recall if this was some old saying, like the wedding saying. Something old, something blue, something something or other.

But I had learned about the three dimensions at school and I had also seen that movie *The Time Machine* where it talked about time as the fourth dimension.

But I had never heard of phasing.

I started to kneel down next to the Todd. "Phasing?" I asked.

Abruptly, Todd got to his feet and stepped back. He moved so quickly, I automatically did the same.

Todd watched the cow, but he spoke to me. "To phase with the vessel. The vessel is off-phase with this phase."

I started to ask if he meant vessel as in blood vessel. It was possible this guy was a veterinarian of sorts.

But before I could ask him to elaborate, a deep hum thickened the air.

Todd took another step back.

I did too.

The cow blinked, not disturbed at all. But the dirt around her hooves was disturbed. Clods shuddered and wobbled. The deep hum made my skull shudder.

Then, with surprising grace, the cow rose up into the air.

She rose and she kept rising. The rope didn't hang down. It drifted in a loose coil right in front of her like a serpent mesmerized by her Happy Meal gaze.

"Hey," I said. Then I said, "Hey."

There was shimmery air above the spot where the cow had stood. It stretched up in a nearly invisible column. Occasional glints of light rose upward, moving a little faster than the cow.

Right after the levitation began, it sped up. In less than a minute, the cow disappeared inside a cloud.

I went over to Todd. "Hey."

He smiled. "How about this weather?"

"What just happened?" I asked.

Todd looked up and shielded his eyes. But he didn't squint. The gesture seemed premeditated. Not natural. It looked like he was saluting the cloud.

Since he wasn't giving me any answers, I decided to dig up the silver beans and get some answers on my own.

But when I took a step, Todd grabbed my arm.

Hard. Like a clamp.

He didn't say anything. He just kept looking up, his grip still painfully latched onto my arm.

I struggled a little and said, "Hey." But that word was getting worn out, so I added. "What's going on?"

Still cloud-gazing, Todd said, "Provisions."

"You mean food?"

"Yes," Todd said. "The foremost has sent me for provisions."

"The foremost?"

"Yes."

"The foremost what?"

Todd glanced at me with some confusion. "He is the Foremost and he sent me for provisions."

Now I could hear the captial F. It was only then I realized what had happened to the other cattle. Whatever was going on involved yanking cows up into the sky.

"You send cows to the Foremost?"

"To the Addendum who then prepares them for the Foremost."

Before I could ask about the identity of the Foremost or the Addendum, the cow came back.

Her descent was only slightly slower than falling, but when she arrived, the landing was gentle. It had all the compassion of releasing a creature back into the wild. Except the cow was on its side and like the others, she was partially dismantled.

The gruesome carcass triggered my adrenalin. I tiwsted out of Todd's grip and grabbed his elbow. Under the brand new workshirt, his arm felt like stone.

He didn't really respond. He didn't pull away. He just turned slightly. But the motion was so unstoppable, he easily broke my grip. Without a word, he knelt next to what was left of the cow.

"No," I said.

I didn't know everything about what had happened during the past few minutes, but one thing I did know—I wasn't going home empty-handed.

I ran around to the other side of the cow and dropped to my knees. I quickly dug the five silver beans from under the carcass. Todd only watched me.

Breathing a little heavy, I got back on my feet and crammed the beans into my pocket. Now, Todd was making his way around the carcass, but I walked quickly backwards, back down the road, wiping the dirt from my hands. "You owe us a cow, Dude."

Todd didn't say anything. He just kept walking toward me.

I turned and ran.

When I looked back, I was a little surprised and a lot relieved to see he wasn't chasing me. He was just standing there watching me.

I yelled at him. "If these things turn out to be worth anything, then maybe we won't call the police." Not that we had a phone.

Todd didn't say anything. He just looked up at the cloud again.

But the cloud had drifted into tatters.

There was nothing up there.

***

When I walked in the door, my mother was humming while she swept the floor. "I've been thinking. Once we sell the cattle, we can look at moving into town and by spring we—"

"Mom."

"In the spring, we'll have a whole different future in front of us."

"Mom."

"I really believe bigger things are coming, Jack."

"Mom."

"What is it, Jack?"

Potato and egg soup sat on the table. She had even set out a little butter. "Mom, I didn't sell the cow."

Her smile fell. "He wouldn't buy our cow?"

"Someone stole the cow, Mom."

"They took it from you?"

"Sort of."

"Are you hurt?"

"No, Mom. But you'll never believe what happened." I could see she was settling into gloom. "Listen, Mom. The cow was stolen, but I did get these." I held out the five silver beans in my dirty palm.

She looked at them with a flat gaze. "Jack."

"These might be worth something." I set the beans on the table one at a time, like coins. But they were still grimed with dirt. They didn't look like much.

She scooped them up, but she didn't look at them. Her mind was too grim to consider them with any real attention. She was too focused on what she was going to do next. Moving to the window, she opened it. "Scrap metal is worthless, Jack." She threw the handful of silver beans outside.

She closed the window. "I'll take one of the cows in tomorrow myself."

She walked past dinner, into her room, and softly shut the door.

The worst part was seeing dinner still on the table, cooling off, uneaten. She had waited for me. She was certainly as hungry as I was, but she had waited for me.

I wasn't sure what I could have done differently. I stared at the candle for a few minutes, before blowing it out well above the next mark.

Before the sun was completely gone, I put a bowl of the stew outside Mom's door with a cloth over it. I decided I should go to bed without dinner. Guilt had always been hungrier than me.

***

It was raining. I opened my eyes. It wasn't a leftover from my dream; it was raining. The roof was hissing and the window was weeping.

I propped himself up on one elbow. We didn't have any clocks in the house. But I could feel that it was after

73

midnight. To me, it always feels like your body doesn't quite belong to you after midnight.

There were no curtains on the window so I could see something was going on outside. Despite the rain, I saw the shimmery air.

I got dressed and slipped out the front door. There was the shimmery column again, with the sparkles and glints rising like pieces of stars.

The rain was warm. Which was kind of weird. It had turned everything to mud. When I squelched over to the shimmer, there was no sign of the beans. They had settled into the muck, apparently close enough to activate each other.

I took another step. I felt the deep hum in my bones.

Whatever the Foremost or the Addendum were, they were sabotaging our livelihood. I thought about going back to the house, getting a large knife, and riding the weird beam up to have a talk with whoever was troubling our lives. But even as I turned to carry out this plan, I knew deep down that I would change my mind before I even reached the steps. I had no idea what was waiting on the other end of this beam.

But when I turned, my left boot wouldn't pull out of the mud and I lost my balance. Just like that, I fell backwards into the shimmer.

I noticed two things right away. First, it was a lot warmer inside the beam. Second, I was lifting off the ground.

The world didn't put up much of a fight for me. The mud let go of my boot and I rose upward. It was like being in an elevator, but without the elevator.

I suppose it would have been a lot more frightening in the daylight. The moon was buried in the storm, so I could barely see anything below as I went up.

Besides, the inside of the shimmery beam was bright green and that made it even harder to see anything outside of it.

The one thing I could still barely see was the horizon, because of the lights of town, and the horizon definitely got lower.

I looked down past my feet. The green shaft of light ended in a tiny black dot.

I looked up. The green shaft led to a brighter green dot.

Todd had said something about a vessel. Todd had been talking about a ship. A spaceship. A flying saucer. A star vessel from another world.

Had to be.

I was just beginning to get a grip on that possibility when I noticed the shimmering green beam suddenly had walls. I continued to rise through the emerald green frog-shine, but I was now inside something like a vertical tunnel made of gray bricks. It was like floating up the inside of a well.

A wishing well, I thought. And that made me the coin.

I didn't expect gray brick walls. That's not the kind of thing you see as far as spaceships and such in movies.

The frog-shine lifted me up into a small room and then turned off. At the same time, there was a loud hiss and the hole beneath me was covered.

I dropped a couple of inches onto both feet.

With the hum of the shimmer gone, I could feel a deep thrum through my feet. Despite the odd look of the walls, I knew I was on a space vessel of some sort.

The room was small, but the ceiling was very high. It had a metal door. The moment my boots touched the floor, the door whispered open.

I walked through, more curious than afraid.

There was so much to take in, I found myself trying to look in every direction at once.

This room was about the size of a school gymnasium, but the ceiling had rounded corners. But even in the curved parts, the walls looked like gray brick.

There was a wild array of machines with the demeanor of kitchen appliances but all of them were very large and all of them seemed to be made by one of those sculptors trying to see how weird they can make art and still call it art. Although the surfaces had probably once been shiny, they were grimy and scuffed, drenched with oily spills. Steam and spices clouded the air.

Beyond that aroma, there was a smell that was very familiar. Without a doubt, the room smelled like something I had smelled before we were poor.

Steak.

Yet the most noticeable thing in the very large room, was the very large woman. She was skinny, but she was extremely tall. She would have had to duck to go through our barn door.

Technically, she wasn't a woman. She had long hair and even though she wore a long gown, I could tell she had the basic contours of a woman.

But everything else—

Like most people, I've seen lots of movies about aliens. This alien didn't look like any of those. This one didn't have any weird beauty. It wasn't gross-out bizarre. This one looked more like what some kid drew during math class. The head looked sort of human, but the eyes were very big ovals, like eggs on end. There was no nose. The mouth was just a line curved into an emotionless frown. No lips.

I froze as she stepped toward me, with the grace of gliding. "AHHH," she said.

Her voice would be found on the lowest keys of a piano. The sound caressed the room. Even though it came from an alien, I could tell it was compassionate. The sound you make when you see a basket of puppies.

She held a pair of tongs and a long knife. She wore a second layer of fabric over the front of her gown. It was made of a thick blue fabric, splotched with blood. A butcher's apron.

She said something to me. It filled the room and ended with what sounded like "V-EYE..."

Her pupils were also shaped like eggs and they were obviously debating whether or not I should be provisions. It was clear to me that standard procedure was to carve whatever came up the beam and prepare it for dinner.

"I'm sorry," I said. It was all that I could come up with in the moment. I backed away from her, also inadvertently moving away from the room I had first entered.

In another part of the ship, something started pounding. Like someone wanting a door to open. But the beat remained firm and steady, more like someone with big feet coming my way.

Whoever the feet belonged to, spoke. It was deeper than the female's voice and it finished with an ominous word that sounded a lot like "D-EYE..."

The female looked over her shoulder and when she looked back at me, her eyes had definitely widened in fright. It was the look of a wife in a bad marriage.

She had to be the Addendum. And whoever was thundering our way was the Foremost.

My body sprang into action before my mind told it to. I threw myself behind something that looked like the offspring of a dishwasher and a Volkswagen bug.

From my hiding place, I saw the female—the Addendum—hurry back behind a steaming counter. She jabbed with her tongs at some unseen business which hissed and spattered.

Someone large entered the room. I didn't peek out. I didn't want to take any chances. I could feel the air in the room making room as it was replaced by the Foremost. I didn't have to get a look to know that he was big.

His voice hit the room like a tsunami. This time his bellow ended with "—FEEE…"

I didn't wait to see if the Addendum would keep me a secret. I scurried behind a row of cannisters and ducked down the first corridor I could find. It wasn't until I was out of the room that it hit me. I didn't have any plan at all. My only thought was to get away from the Foremost.

The passage was big of course and also rounded at the top and also made of gray bricks. Even though I was sprinting for my life, curiosity made me run my fingertips along the wall. It didn't have the grainy texture of bricks. It was smooth like metal.

Then it also hit me. I had probably just taken the corridor the Foremost had come out of.

I was even more sure about that when I saw where the corridor led.

This room had very large upholstered chairs. There wasn't much light, but the console in front of the chairs blinked and held dazzling screens. Just past the console was an incredible view.

I think in the back of my mind, I had been hoping the vessel was only drifting in the stratosphere. But I was way above that.

I was in outer space. The earth still filled most of the view. But almost everything else was stars. Stars and stars, forever and ever.

Cutting across the field of stars was something like a diagonal gash that must have been many miles long. It looked like someone had torn the constellations. It was a gap in space with the rough edges of a wound. Looking into it was like looking down into the eerie depth of a ravine.

I knew right away. It was the Quantum Fracture.

They had said the Annihilation Engine had caused some slight side-effects. But this had injured reality. The vessel I was standing in had probably come out of that wound. As I stood there in the cockpit, I wondered why the authorities or anyone hadn't noticed this thing floating just above the world.

Then I remembered the fifth bean. "And one for phasing," Todd had said.

This vessel was phased out of human sight or something. No one even knew it was up here. I couldn't help but wonder how many other creepy intruders had bled out of the Quantum Fracture.

I had never felt so small.

I had to find a way to get back home. If the Foremost found me he might smash me with a fist the size of a hippopotamus or just toss me in an airlock thing and let it spit me out into the stars and stars and stars. Based on the fact that he was gnawing on our cows without permission, I didn't think he would be up for a diplomatic visit.

Hands shaking, I stepped up to the console and studied it closely. I guess I was hoping to spot a button that looked like the down button on an elevator.

No such luck. I probably would have just stood there hypnotized by all the controls until the Foremost found me, except that I decided to think out loud, "There's got to be a way."

"Hello, there," someone said.

I sprang sideways, preparing to be snatched up and snuffed out. I slammed into metal. Pain flared up my arm.

But this voice didn't boom. This voice was human-sized and it spoke English.

Clutching my arm, I turned to see Todd standing in the gloom.

He still wore the brand-new overalls and brand-new boots. "It is a pleasure to meet you," he said.

I was disappointed in myself that I hadn't figured him out sooner. "Are you an android?"

"Yes," Todd replied immediately.

"You were built to look like one of us and sent down to get provisions."

"Yes," Todd replied. "Meat." The android took a few steps closer. "You're bleeding."

I poked through the tear in my shirt. My finger came away with a streak of red. I'd cut myself pretty good.

Todd seemed ready to answer any questions, so I asked, "Listen, can you get me off this ship?"

"Yes."

It suddenly dawned on me my general request could end with bad loopholes, so I got more specific. "Can you get me off this vessel alive? The way you get the provisions up here. Can you use that to get me back down safely? Alive? In one piece? Alive?"

"Yes," Todd said, but he didn't move.

"Okay," I said slowly. "Please get me off this vessel in one piece alive—and without being seen by the male or female," I added quickly.

Todd didn't respond.

"Without being seen by the Foremost or the Addendum," I added.

"Yes," Todd said and led the way out a different corridor.

Following Todd, I started to feel hopeful. After seeing the Quantum Fracture, it was comforting to be with someone else who was small and insignificant just like me, even if that person wasn't technically a person.

We hadn't gone far before the ship began to pound again. The footsteps of the Foremost. The voice roared and ended with "...F-EYE..."

I whispered in terror. "Is he looking for me?"

Todd pitched his voice a little lower and spoke very distinctly. He was translating. 'The sentient is leaving footprints."

Footprints.

I looked down and I could have kicked myself. My boots were still covered in mud. I looked back down the corridor. I might as well have left a trail of bread crumbs. This was more like leaving a trail of donuts.

The air in the passage moved past us. The Foremost had reached the cockpit. His voice resounded and something nearby, a loose piece in the wall, rattled. The final word with a prolonged "...FUMMM..."

"Blood," Todd translated. "There's blood here. Not from the provisions. From the sentient."

"Let's go!" I whispered.

We went.

The Foremost thundered.

"Where is the android," Todd translated. Then just like that, Todd turned around and called out. "I'm right here."

Now the Foremost was enthusiastic. His footsteps sounded like someone was shooting the vessel with an old-fashioned cannon, over and over.

"Go, go!" I prodded Todd.

He went, and within moments we burst back into the kitchen. The Addendum stepped out from behind the gargantuan grill and spoke.

"What might you taste like," Todd translated for her.

I used Todd like a shield and shoved past her, barely slipping past her slender fingers as they tried to collect me.

I pushed Todd into the small room where the beam had first brought me. "Shut the door," I said. "Shut the door. Shut the door and lock it."

Todd closed his eyes and the door whispered shut with a click.

Someone slammed into the door. Stumbling onto the spot where I had first arrived, I shouted at Todd. "Open the beam, Todd. Open it. Open it fast. Down. Down."

Todd stood next to me and closed his eyes. Like a genie.

The well opened and side by side, we dropped into the green light.

The gray bricks flashed by and in another minute or two, I could see wisps of clouds rising as we passed them, on our way back down.

We were moving fast, but not fast enough. I knew that any moment, the Foremost would reverse the beam.

I panicked. "Todd, we need to go down faster! As fast as possible!"

Even as the words fell out of my mouth, I realized I had just made a huge mistake.

Todd closed his eyes and the beam vanished.

Fortunately, we had already entered the atmosphere. Unfortunately, there was still a lot of atmosphere left.

Todd and I fell.

I have to admit, for the first minute or so, I just screamed. But after two or three good screams, my lungs felt almost frozen, so I stopped.

The roar of the darkness took over.

I was as good as dead, but I tried to control my fall. Call it stubborn self-preservation. I used my hands like fins, reaching and sweeping at the air, trying to shape my descent, until I was freefalling just like a skydiver. Except without a parachute.

There was the faintest of light along the edge of the world. Todd tumbled slowly nearby, floppy as a scarecrow. His eyes glanced here and there, uninterested.

When we fell through the last of the clouds, I had an amazing view of my small part of the world. A splinter of the moon perched above the dark horizon. It wasn't long before I saw the barn, the little dots of sleeping cattle, and the house. The house I was born in. And based on my current trajectory, it would also be the house I died in.

Screaming hadn't changed anything. I forced myself to control my gasps of terror. As my world moved closer, I decided I should use my time as best as I could. The thing about falling from such a height, you have plenty of time to think.

Of all things, I thought of Mom's candles. In my mind, my last moments were measured in wax. That meant I only had a fraction of an inch to live. Or maybe one paragraph in a half-a-book.

The beam reappeared, the shimmery air less than a yard away.

Desperate, I dog-paddled toward it. I could continue to fall to certain death or get inside the beam and rise up to most-likely death. Of course, if I ended up being prepped for a pan, I might be wishing I was back here, hurtling to an instant grave.

I snatched at the beam with both hands. It was like trying to grab onto a waterfall that was falling up. It tugged against my fingers. I was already feeling the relief I would feel once I was back inside the beam.

I reached in farther, up to my elbows and I started to slow down. That's when it hit me that I might have another option.

Instead of trying to crawl into the beam, I cupped my hands so I dragged harder against the flow. I also touched the edge of the beam with the toes of my boots to steady my position. I wasn't really falling anymore.

This was more like sliding down one of those poles that firemen used to have.

I had just gotten the hang of it when I saw my house coming up fast. In a panic, I stuck my arms in farther. Too far.

The beam wrenched me to a stop. It got a better grip on me and I started to rise, fast. As it lifted me, it also started to pull me in.

Struggling, I threw myself backwards as hard as I could and fell out into the night again.

Turning in midair, I tried to land on my feet, but I merely sprawled face first in the mud.

Sitting up, I scraped the muck of my eyes just in time to see the front door fly open. My mother blinked at the feeble morning. "Jack. What are you—"

I wobbled onto my feet, turning in a full circle as I tried to get my balance. There was Todd in a Todd-shaped crater. His eyes twitched and found me. "Hello there," he said. "It's a pleasure to meet you." His overalls didn't look new anymore.

My mother's voice shook. "Jack, are you all right? Who is that?"

My head spun and I fell to one knee. My body was still adjusting to the shock of falling for so long and still being alive. "Mom, the cows--" I started, but I was distracted by the hum of the beam.

The hum was different. It sounded deeper. Thicker.

Now that my head was clearing I knew the beam had been sounding different for some time now. Stunned by my survival, I just hadn't noticed.

I staggered toward the shimmering air. It definitely sounded different. And it looked different. The sparkles and glimmers weren't going up. They were going down.

I whirled around. "Mom, get back in the house. Something's coming."

Her eyes were wide. "What? What is it, Jack?"

I ran up the steps and gently pushed her inside. "Bigger things." I slammed the door.

Hurrying back out across the mud, I took a close look at the beam. It was definitely moving down. The Foremost had given up trying to bring me back. He was coming to get me. And when he got me, he might just get my mom and maybe the whole town. Whatever the

Quantum Fracture had allowed to arrive on the edge of the world, I had put out the welcome mat.

I faced the house. We didn't have a welcome mat. We had rickety wooden steps that led to a crooked door. Next to the crooked door was the shovel.

Even as I ran for the steps, I could hear the beam drop to a deeper tone. I was guessing this was because it was carrying something huge.

I grabbed at the shovel, but I was in too big of a hurry. My fingertips glanced off the handle and it fell off the steps into the mud. Trying to hold down my panic, I leapt after it and tripped over the handle.

The beam sang a note that was so deep I could feel it more than hear it.

Grabbing the shovel, I slogged back to the beam.

I wiped my hands on my pants, got a good grip on the handle and dug into the world.

I gouged up the heavy mud. I worked frantically, but I couldn't find any of the beans. The rain or their own power had planted them farther down, anchoring the beam.

I had no other plan, so I just kept digging. And when I finally saw a glint of silver, I dropped to my knees and clawed it out with my bare hands.

I was prepared to pry out all five, but just taking out one did the trick.

The humming stopped. The beam vanished.

Exhausted down to my bones, I collapsed and let the mud soothe the side of my face. The whole nightmare was finally over.

But it wasn't.

I rolled onto my back and in the growing glow of dawn, way up in the sky, I saw the Foremost. His arms and legs were spread out. He grabbed at the air. He worked his legs like someone in a race. He roared with fury.

He was big and getting bigger.

I tried to get up, but I fell on my face again. My boots had trouble digging in. For a horrible moment, all I did was scurry in the mud, going nowhere.

The shovel saved me again. This time I used it more like I was pole vaulting. I reached the steps, threw the shovel aside, and scrambled up to the door. "Mom!"

She opened the door and we collided. But I was able to keep both of us on our feet, as I flung the two of us over to the fireplace, away from the door.

The sound of the Foremost becoming the Former was kind of like an explosion. Like very loud and very brief thunder.

The front of our house vaporized into splinters, pieces of the door bouncing off my back as I shielded Mom.

After a few seconds, making sure the roof was still going to stay up, I stood up straight and held onto Mom until I was sure she could stand on her own.

She looked at me, terrified. I patted her on the shoulder and went to see.

The Foremost had landed face down. He had landed so hard I could see dry rocky soil around him. His hand, which was about the size of a cow, had hit the front steps, destroying most of the front of the house.

I stood there and watched him.

There was only a little blood. But there was definitely no breath.

***

I didn't tell anybody anything until that afternoon. That gave me time to use my father's shovel to tunnel under the body and get the other four beans.

It took hours. Every once in a while, Todd said it was a pleasure to meet me.

Then I went into town, told everyone what happened, and came home.

When people started showing up to see if I was lying, they got a good look and went back to town to tell more people. More people came. And more.

Scientists and other authority types were eager to collect the body. For the sake of research, but also for the sake of everyone's noses.

They took Todd too. He was still chatting the last I saw him.

A few days later, some of the people in town patched up our place enough to make do.

A week later, I sold what remained of our cattle and we moved into town.

Two weeks later, I sold our land.

A month later, I walked into the university with a lawyer watching over me and I showed the scientists the beans. I had kept them hidden in the tool box.

A year later, my mother and I were financially comfortable.

I still have the tool box. I still have the shovel.

Last week, Mom made me a birthday cake. We can afford a hundred birthday cakes now, but she said she wanted to make one for me. I have to admit I kind of got choked up when I saw she had marked all the candles with a Sharpie.

I told her I was going to write all this down. Everything that happened. I said that since Silver Bean Enterprises is doing so well on Wall Street, I might call it "Jack and the Bean Stock." But Mom said people might not take it very seriously.

She said they might think all of this was a fairy tale.

But sometimes I pick up that half-a-book and I like to think that maybe, that's exactly what it was.

ALBERT BOLIDE SPICULE BATTLES ARCHITEUTHIS DUX
BY ERIK PETERSON

Alright, little Kiu-Kiu, that's enough stalling. It's time for bed.

Sure, I can turn on the sky for you. Oh, it looks a little overcast, though. Want me to replay last night? There. Wow, the moons were beautiful last night, weren't they? Look how bright they are.

You know which moon's my favorite?

That's right! Archie.

I guess it is a silly name for a moon. But do you know what it's really called? Architeuthis Dux.

No, no, I'm not joking. Architeuthis Dux. Do you know why they call it that? Well, you see how those bright little squiggles go from the light side to the dark side? Those are *giant* mountain ranges that poke up just high enough over the horizon to stay lit longer than the dark parts below them. But from here they look like tentacles don't they? When it's a half moon or quarter moon, it looks like a squid swimming through the sky. And that's what Architeuthis Dux means, in one of the dead languages. Giant Squid.

Well, squids might be real. There are lots of legends about them. In the stories they live in space, trying to catch ships and cruisers. But those might just be stories. Nothing can live in the vacuum of space that isn't in hibernation or inside a ship. And space is so big, if a squid were floating around out there somewhere, the ships are so few and far between that they'd never find a meal!

Well, aren't you clever. I guess you're right. If there were lots of squids and leviathans and other space monsters out there, I guess they could all eat each other to say alive. And, you know what? Maybe they stay away from ships because they learned their lesson from the early starfarers like Albert Bolide Spicule.

What? You haven't heard of Bolide? Well, I have failed in my duties as your parent. Bolide was the cleverest, toughest, spunkiest starfarer ever to warp spacetime. He would ride comets for fun and floss his teeth with superstrings. I've even heard the asteroid belt around Undriata is where planets used to come to play chicken with him, and those rocks are all that's left.

Okay, okay, let me see what I can remember.

Now nobody knows for sure, but people say 'farers who flew with 'farers who flew with Bolide claimed that he wasn't even from our universe as we know it. When he was just a little boy living in some back fold of some 82nd level higher dimension, he was too curious for his own good, and as easy as a baby like your little brother might knock over a tube of crumbernuts, Bolide wriggled his way into our universe and liked it so much he decided to stay.

When he was just eight years old, he found his way to a ship in Sol port. A little eight year old boy walked past all the hands and the scientists and the colonists, right up to the captain.

"Permission to come aboard, sir?" asked the boy.

The captain brushed him off. "Colonist registration is that way. Go get your mom to help you."

But Bolide persisted. "I don't want to be a

colonist, sir. I want to serve on your crew."

The captain laughed, and so did the men he was talking to.

Bolide still persisted. "Captain, if you're so sure it's silly how about we make a little wager?"

"What wager would I possibly want to make with a kid?"

"Would it be worth your while if I could show you how to make your warp arcs tighter?"

The Captain laughed again. "Boy, this ship has the best navigators in the Milky Way. If there's a fraction of a degree to be wrenched into a warp arc, these boys have clamped it down."

"Then that's the bet," said Bolide. "Give me five minutes with the nav computer. If I can get your warp arc a half a degree tighter, you let me on your crew."

"Well," said the Captain, "if this isn't the craziest way I've ever seen a lad try to get a free tour of the bridge."

"Bridge?" said the boy. "I'd have thought the captain of a ship like this would carry an interface with him everywhere. Maybe I should go find a vessel that knows what it's doing."

There was no laughter at that, because now the joke wasn't on the boy, it was on the captain, and nobody wanted to laugh at the captain.

So, the captain squatted down next to the boy and pulled up a display in the air between them. He swirled a few icons and changed a few settings and said, "There, kid. You've got a simulation of the navigation program. Knock yourself out." And he went back to talking with his men.

But that conversation didn't last, because within thirty seconds, the captain couldn't hold his men's attention. Because right there, in that port, Bolide was introducing the world to the flux field, where the actual movement of the ship gives the space warp an extra half a degree of flux, which within a few years would be standard operating procedure for every 'farer in the galaxy. It's the very system your ancestors used to come to this planet.

The captain had no choice but to honor his wager and let the boy come aboard. It's said the reason that healthy 'farers are classified as "able bodied" is because

Bolide signed into the ship's computers that day as Spicule, A. B.

Now as Bolide grew up, he became the most popular and sought after 'farer in the galaxy. He was so capable and commanding that no ship was big enough to hold all the crew and cargo and passengers. So they had to make him the biggest ship ever built. A ship so big that when it flew between Saturn and Uranus it had to fold in its ramscoops so they didn't catch on any planetary rings.

Bolide would brave any solar weather and navigate any treacherous stretch of space debris. There was no span of galaxy too intimidating, too new, or too unknown to steer him off.

Now one day, Bolide heard about some ships being afraid to head down around Sagittarius A, so naturally, he couldn't keep himself away.

As I said before, space is mighty big. And looking for something in space can be tough, especially when you don't know where it is or what you're looking for. But for as big as Bolide's ship was, it was just as fast, and they shot up and down that whole sector, sending out radio signals and listening for responses, with all ansible frequencies open, listening for distress calls. And pretty soon, can you guess what he found?

It was the biggest space squid anyone had ever seen. It was big enough to gobble up gas giants like Jupiter and wash them down with watery planets like old Earth itself. Massive tentacles spiraled off it, still juggling the bits of the ships it had crushed the way your uncle juggles packets of powdered juice at family picnics.

Now the crew of the ship was ready to run, but Bolide told them to hold their ground. "Have I ever let you down?" he said with a grin. "I am Albert Bolide Spicule, and I will bring you home alive. But first we've got to make this area safe again. Get me the fastest shuttle we've got."

The crew trusted Bolide, and they brought him the fastest shuttle they could find and the best pilot. But Bolide waved the pilot away. "No offense, son, I'm sure you're great. But I'd rather face that space squid than face the momma of the man I sent off to fight such a creature as that." And Bolide took the controls himself.

"Leave the bay door open," he said, as he flew out of the side of the ship.   He swooped out past the monster, blasting it in the eyes to get its attention. His little shuttle was just a tiny annoyance to that big squid, so Bolide set out to make himself as annoying as possible.   He blasted barnacles off the creature's tentacles the size of moons, and he took shots at nooks the size of Reobald Canyon and crannies the size of DuFrense crater that he figured must be the creature's sensitive spots.

Before too long, he had that squid enraged.   It swatted at him and grabbed for him, but Bolide was too quick.   He ducked in and out of those tentacles like when you and your friends play in the high roots of the river trees during the dry season.

And then, all of the sudden, he made a beeline back for the ship. He flew straight as an arrow as fast as he could.   One long tentacle shot out after him, going almost as fast as he was.

The crew called to him over the radio. "Sir, what are you doing?"

"When I give the order, close the bay door."

"Sir, the bay door is huge. At the speed you're going, even if we close it now, you'd be in before it finished closing. And it would be a close call on the tentacle."

"I don't want to keep the tentacle out, son," Bolide said. "I want to catch it."

When the moment was right, he shouted, "Now!" And they started closing the bay door. Bolide slid into the port.

But much to the surprise of the men waiting for him, he did not land. He arced his ship back up towards the closing bay door.

The tentacle came in after him.

But just as it was starting to search around, Bolide landed on the wall of the bay door itself, the shuttle's nose pointing down towards the tentacle. He dug the heavy clamps of the shuttle's rough surface landing gear into the metal of the door. And then he fired up his warp engines, full throttle.

The shuttle slammed that big heavy bay door, clamping down on the end of the tentacle, pinching it like a starving ooglak baby biting down on your finger.

"Hit the boosters!" Bolide shouted. "Now!"

The giant space squid pulled, but the ship pulled back.

Then Bolide, sure that the shuttle would rip away from the bay door, grabbed the personal rocket pack off one of the space suits, scrambled out of the shuttle, and secured it to the shuttle's landing gear. He turned the rocket pack on, using it to hold the landing gear to the bay door the same way the fired-up shuttle held the bay doors closed.

Just then the squid gave a giant yank and the entire ship lurched towards the beast. But the ship righted itself and began to pull back again, and as the crew tried to figure out who had had the presence of mind to get to the controls so quickly, they realized Bolide was on the bridge with them. He'd somehow made his way from the shuttle bay in a couple of eye blinks. The 'farers that saw it, swear it was like he materialized out of the deck itself, right at the helm.

"I've got this," said Bolide.

And that started the wildest tug-of-war that has ever been had by man or beast. That ship was big, and it was strong, but that monster was even bigger and even stronger. It thrashed about space trying to get free.

Now Bolide knew this whole galaxy as well as any man. And he knew that as dangerous as that giant squid was, there was one thing in that section of space that was even bigger and meaner. And I'll bet you can guess what that was.

See? You're as clever as Bolide. There's a great big black hole at Sagittarius A. That monster roiled and reeled so much that pretty soon, it wandered where it really shouldn't have. And the next thing that squid knew, it was getting sucked down, down into that inky maw like a whirlpool.

Bolide's ship followed, getting spun around faster and faster like a rock on the end of a string, but also getting pulled in after that giant space squid.

All over the ship, the force of the spinning became more powerful than the gravitational generators. The crew on the bridge had to cling to their controls to keep from being drug across the deck. The crew running for their lives down the corridors had to run along the walls instead of the deck. The crew in the galley moved their tables and chairs off the floor onto the walls so they could carry on eating.

"Set up a warp!" Bolide yelled to his men. "Use our speed to help with the flux field! And when I give the order, let go of the monster!"

Bolide's crew must have been very loyal indeed, because they held on far longer than any group of rational men could ever have been expected to hold onto a giant space monster that was being sucked into a black hole. But those men were loyal, and they trusted their captain, and they stood their ground as the whole ship trembled as the monster pulled them in deeper and deeper, and their ship went around and around--

"Now!" screamed Bolide.

The men opened the bay door. The tentacle flew out. The centripetal force shot that ship away from the monster, and away from the black hole. They made good distance, but after a moment, they could already feel the black hole pulling against them.

"Activate warp! And the flux field! The flux field!"

The ship took off through the warp in space-time

as the last bits of the monster were dragged into the black hole, never to be heard from again.

Albert Bolide Spicule, on the other hand, well, he was still heard from plenty. I'll bet it might just be on account of him that all the space squids and beasties have all gone into hiding. The tales they tell of his adventures--

No, no. It's late and you've got to upload to school in the morning, so that's probably enough for now.

Sleep tight, Kiu-kiu.

And don't go joining any starfarer ships without asking first, you hear?

#

THE SEVENTH GIFT
BY CJ WEST

The ones who made me gave me seven gifts.
The first was a perfect physical form.
Strength, health, symmetry—what many call
beauty.

The cords tangled over the Oracle's dais like a thicket of briars, running from the machines that spun and whirred in a semi-circle around the marble slab. Reyu marveled at it from behind the glass in the antechamber. All this to keep her alive. He'd never realized.

He couldn't see her, raised as if in a tower above the line of robed acolytes. Anticipation burned through him. All the images of the Oracle showed her as she was before she entered stasis: a young woman of thirty-five, tall and stately, golden hair flowing long and loose down her back. In the images, her chin always tilted up and her deep brown eyes peered off into the distance, seeing the future and the right course. In the images, she looked like a queen.

And she was a queen, created solely for the purpose of leading, given seven gifts to help her do so. Beauty, character, persuasion, grace, intelligence, love—and the last. Eternal sleep. So her soul could continue to lead as her body slept.

The line moved forward, and Reyu stepped past the glass partition, the doors sliding silently open to admit him into the Oracle's chamber. His breath caught as the air around him thrummed with the pulse of machinery. He had worked so long and hard for this—passing up through the ranks of acolytes, serving and studying. And now he would take the test. If he passed, he would wear the helm of the high priests. He would hear her voice and deliver it to the people.

It was not so impossible a thought, no matter what Nikko said.

"You won't hear her voice, Reyu. No one does." His brother's voice this morning had been derisive. He'd come to visit Reyu in the acolyte rooms. Nikko had never liked the idea of Reyu in the priesthood, so it shouldn't have shocked him when Nikko came—on this of all days—to persuade him to leave the temple.

"You won't hear it, but they'll convince you to keep serving them anyway. They'll keep you bowing and scraping forever, just like the rest of us. This all has to stop, don't you see? Walk away from it. Come home."

Home. As if that hovel in the city's outer rings were still Reyu's home. No—he belonged here at the temple, near the Oracle.

Nikko's bitter words worried Reyu, even as they angered him. If the Monitors heard Nikko's seditious words, they would arrest him and send him to the camps. Why could Nikko not embrace faith? At least he only spoke this way to Reyu.

Reyu closed his eyes, pushing the confrontation with his brother from his mind. Nikko's doubts would be assuaged once Reyu heard the Oracle's voice. Then Nikko would have to believe.

Only a few more acolytes ahead of him now. His friend Anath knelt before the dais, his white robes blending with the white marble, and the head priestess approached with the helm. The elderly woman wore the golden robes of the Inner Circle, her white hair twisted in ornate braids around her head. She held the golden circlet over Anath's head, drawing out the moment, before slowly lowering it onto his brow. Anath's face was a mirror of Reyu's heart—hope and anxiety mingling into something that looked like rapture.

Moments passed and Reyu's heart beat hard. Did he want his friend to pass, or to fail? If Anath passed, would that mean less chance for Reyu? He shook his head, fighting the selfish thought. It was beneath a priest of the Oracle.

The priestess stepped forward and removed the helm from Anath's brow. Anath stood, shoulders drooped, and Bray, the head of the acolytes, beckoned him toward the door on the left of the chamber. Reyu breathed a shaky sigh. His heart sank for his friend. Anath had wanted this nearly as much as Reyu. In an entire class of acolytes, only two or three would hear the

Oracle's voice and be invited into the inner circle. So far, from his class, only one had been chosen.

Just two more, then it would be his turn. He closed his eyes—he would not watch these next two—and mentally rehearsed his supplication in the old language.

If he was a fit vessel, the Oracle would know. She would speak to him. He need not worry.

A tap on his shoulder prodded him forward twice, and then it was his turn. He opened his eyes and walked toward the marble slab. He climbed the gleaming steps, the rapture building to a crescendo in his chest. Finally—he stood before her. She was the most beautiful woman he had ever seen. Dark, thick eyelashes fanned out over her smooth, amber skin, and her red lips parted just slightly, holy breath moving through them. Her hair fell over her shoulders in gentle waves. She was beautiful and strong, wise and terrible. She was no queen—she was a god.

Overcome, he knelt, nearly forgetting his purpose until the cold metal helm slipped over his brow.

The words of the old language poured through his mind, his own voice intoning a prayer for only the Oracle to hear.

I am your servant. Speak, and let me hear your voice. I will serve you all the days of my life and bring your word to my people. Only let me hear you.

He forced his mind to quiet, straining to keep it blank, open. The machines throbbed, and the robes of the other hopeful acolytes rustled. But he heard no voice.

Please. The old language was comfortable in his mind. He had studied it for so long, practiced its odd sounds, its strange rhythms, it came as easily to him as his first language. *I wish only to serve you, to be acceptable in your sight. If I am not acceptable now, see me for what I may become.*

His pulse pounded counter to the machines, and the dissonance highlighted the anxiety within him. *Please. If not for me, for my family. My brother . . . he needs faith.*

Warm fingers pressed at his temples.

Please.

The helm lifted off his brow, leaving him feeling too light, too weak as he rose and walked toward Bray.

<< *Please.* >>

Reyu's eyes shot open in awe. That voice in his mind—it wasn't his own.

The second gift was control of passions.
A temperament fit for a ruler.

"Not all are attuned to the voice of the Oracle." Bray pressed his dry, papery hand over Reyu's as he passed through the door. "Do not grieve."

"But—holiness." Reyu's voice was hoarse. It felt wrong in his throat, the words awkward.

Bray placed his arm over Reyu's shoulder, steering him down the hall. Their feet scraped against the metal grate of the walkway. "Your dedication is to be commended, Reyu. Do not look at this as a rejection. It is merely a release from higher duty. Your service is still needed here at the temple."

"I heard her."

Bray stopped, turning to Reyu with a clouded expression. "What's this?"

"I heard her, holiness." The joy of it bubbled through him. He'd heard her—the Oracle. What he'd been hoping for all his life. He'd heard her.

Bray shook his head. "No, young one." He pointed to the helm on his brow. "If you had heard her, we would all have known. When she speaks to one, she speaks to all."

"But—"

Bray patted him on the shoulder. "It happens sometimes. You wanted so badly to hear her voice, you imagined it."

The joy crumpled into confusion. That voice—it had seemed so clear. So distinct. Could he have imagined it?

They had reached the fork in the hallway—the left fork leading back to the acolyte rooms, the right to the high priests' quarters. Bray gently pressed him toward the left. "Out of curiosity," he said. "What did you think she said to you?"

"She said . . . please."

The third gift was the skill of gentle persuasion.

Reyu could not go to his rooms. He couldn't look the other failed acolytes in the eye, not while this confusion reigned inside him. He had heard her . . . hadn't he? Her voice—it had been soft. He could not have imagined that. But then, why had the other priests not heard it, too?

He left the temple, its metal walkways giving way to cobbled stone streets. Domed clay buildings spread out below him, filling the downward slope of the city. He'd never really looked at it from this perspective before. He'd barely come out of the temple since entering it two years before—he'd been so dedicated to studying the old language and the Precepts. Seeing the city now, in the red light of the setting sun, it suddenly looked like a wasps' nest, clumping against the side of the mountain.

Reyu walked, water porters ducking out of his way. Even acolytes were given deference.

Lest the Monitors were watching.

No, that was Nikko's voice, Nikko's bitterness. Reyu believed. He'd always believed. The Oracle's voice brought peace, her mandates created order. The Monitors upheld her law, and the people prospered under their watch.

Except for the dissenters.

Reyu's steps quickened. He needed to get to his brother. Nikko must stop this talk of his. Reyu had been hoping to come to him with the persuasion of proof, but now he would have to rely on the influence of his own faith. He had not spent enough time with his brother these last two years, and without his guidance, Nikko had lost his way.

Nikko needed him.

He arrived as the first moon was rising, its sister trailing behind on the horizon, and pushed past the cloth draped over the doorway. Its once bright stripes were faded and dingy. Nikko knelt by the fire, stoking it in preparation for the evening meal. When they were young, people had often mistaken them for twins. The same curling brown hair, the same stocky build, the same crooked smile. They could never tell that Reyu was the older brother.

He blinked in the dark light of the hovel, feeling awkward and foolish—like a man wearing clothes meant for a boy. Why had he come here?

"Where is Ma?" he asked, for something to say. "And Havel?"

"Fetching water." Nikko stood, brushing soot from his hands. "Will you stay for dinner?"

Reyu nodded, hesitant. Nikko jutted his chin toward the table, where a small pile of potatoes waited. They pulled out stools and began peeling. The scrape of knives on hard roots filled the silence for a while.

"So," Nikko said. "You heard nothing."

It wasn't a question, so Reyu didn't answer.

"If the old hag was going to speak to anyone, she'd have spoken to you. Surely, you see the truth now."

Reyu's hands froze, a long, twisting peel hanging suspended from his knife. "Nikko, you can't say things like that. You'll cause trouble."

"Exactly what we need to be doing." Nikko's voice strained with exasperation. "You've studied the old language, the old texts. You've lived in the temple! You've seen what we used to be able to do, the *technology*—" He said that last in the old language; it had no modern translation. "We are capable of so much more, but the priests are so worried about maintaining their power, their hold on us through their false Oracle—"

Reyu let out a panicked whine and Nikko stopped, sighing. "Reyu, you have to face it. If the Oracle doesn't order it, we don't do it. And what does the Oracle demand? That we mine—and send all our ore off world. Who profits from that? Only the priests. They control the portal, they get the wealth. But no one can question them, no one can call them on it, or the Monitors will be on them like flies on a carcass."

"Hush," Reyu dropped his potato and gripped Nikko's arm. "Don't you think of anyone but yourself? If the Monitors hear of this, you'll be arrested. What will happen to Ma and Havel? Think, Nikko!"

Nikko shook his head. "I can't stay quiet about this. That Oracle is a fraud. If we're all too afraid to say it out loud, we'll never get out from under her thumb. People need to wake up, they need to question."

"You've spoken to others," Reyu said, realizing the truth. This passion in Nikko did not appear overnight. It had been building. And he hadn't had Reyu to balance him—to listen to him. He'd found someone else.

"There are others who think like me. There's a group of us, and we're going to change things. Reyu, now that you know—"

Reyu stood, knocking his stool to the floor. "No."

"You can help. With your knowledge of the temple and the priests, our cause can succeed."

"No. Nikko, we have to get you out of here. Secrets like this don't stay hidden." He rushed to the cabinets. So bare. What could Nikko take? There had to be something that could keep him alive for a few days, a week maybe, until Reyu could—

"I'm not leaving. I won't run."

Reyu turned to his brother, eyes narrowed. "They'll *arrest you.*"

"I know." Nikko nodded. "At the trial, I'll say my piece. They may kill me for it, but the whispers will grow. The Monitors can't silence everyone. We need doubt."

"We need faith." Reyu gripped him by the arm. He wanted to shake him, make him stop this. But Nikko's jaw was set. He watched the door as if . . .

"They're coming here, aren't they? You knew— that's why you came this morning. Why didn't you say?"

Nikko pulled him into an embrace, shocking Reyu into silence. How long had it been since his brother hugged him? "You'll finish this, brother. I don't believe in much, but I believe in you."

Footsteps sounded on the stone outside. Too many to be their mother and sister. Too many to be their neighbors.

"Open. In the name of the Oracle."

Nikko squared his shoulders and walked past Reyu to the door, pushing aside the cloth. He offered his hands for the Monitors to bind. They added a gag, and dragged him away.

Reyu could only follow behind as his brother disappeared up the sloping city streets.

Fourth, they gave me grace.
The capacity to forgive.
Did you know that was a genetic trait?

Nikko was taken to the city square and forced to his knees. They sliced his head from his neck with a stone ax.

A nimble mind was the fifth gift.
An intellect that danced, like a flower in the wind.

Reyu could not go home. What could he tell Ma and Havel? Were they arriving home even now, with water on their backs, ready to boil the potatoes, only to find them half peeled on the table? How could he tell them that Nikko was not coming home? That Reyu had failed him?

He walked the city until the first moon had set, her pale sister the only light left in the sky. No matter how far he wandered, he could not escape the image of Nikko in the city square, bound and gagged.

There was no trial. At a trial, Nikko would have been able to speak. His words would have had an opportunity to persuade people, to influence them. No. That wasn't why. That was Nikko's bitterness seeping into Reyu's heart again. There was no trial because no trial was necessary. Nikko's own words condemned him.

In the dark, every slap of his sandals on the stone brought sharp remembrance of the stone ax against Nikko's neck.

A stone ax.

Nikko was right. Reyu had read the old texts. He'd seen the *technology* depicted in them—running water, *electric* lights, metals. Weapons that far surpassed stone axes. The priests taught that these *technologies* were holy, available only to super humans like the Oracle, who was created for greatness. But—humanity had once had the capacity to create that greatness. They had made the Oracle, hadn't they?

Their ancestors had developed these secrets. They had sent their children across the galaxy to new worlds. Why did it stop? Why did it . . . go backward?

Reyu raked his hands over his face, heart filling with anguish. These were Nikko's doubts, not his. He did not want them. He turned to face the temple—the only metal in the city. It gleamed in the sister's weak light.

The Oracle was within. She had spoken to him. Beneath his grief, her voice was still there.

The Oracle could soothe him. He turned his steps toward the temple. He must end this agony of doubt.

Sixth, I was gifted a love of humanity.
Their ways would speak to my soul
like music.

Reyu passed through the doors of the temple, no simple cloth covering, but metal doors that whooshed open with the wave of a hand. How had he never thought of this before? The gleaming metal of the walls, the marble of the dais, the *glass*. He'd always found these things mystical, holy. But Nikko's doubts clamored in his mind.

If these were humanity's birthright, and not holy relics out of reach, then why did the priests keep them from the people? Why did the Oracle not teach them? If she was placed in her perpetual sleep to lead them, why did she not lead them to something better?

He stopped at the dining hall, watching silently from the shadows as the priests in their ornate robes feasted on piles of food, roasted meats and baked delicacies. While his brother's blood still ran in the streets. While his mother and sister ate potatoes in the darkness.

This wealth—it came from the mines. The mines the Oracle commanded the people to work. The priests delivered the ore off world, as Nikko said, through a portal they did not understand nor seek to understand. As long as it brought them wealth, and they kept their control over the people below them. Could the priests really be so shortsighted?

No. Reyu knew these people, good men and women. Those who wore the helm were holy. They heard the Oracle's voice. And if the Oracle commanded them to do these things, it was because she was wise beyond their capacity to understand. Nikko didn't understand this.

But...

Reyu could not quiet the voice of dissent. It haunted him all the way down the long hallway, past the acolyte rooms and forking down to the Oracle's dais.

The antechamber was empty—and Reyu could see through the glass that the chamber was empty as well. The priests felt no need to guard the Oracle. Anyone who would threaten her was found and silenced quickly, as Nikko had been. Reyu pushed past the crush of pain in his heart and approached the dais.

The machines hummed around him as he climbed the marble steps and looked down on the beautiful sleeping woman. For the second time that night, he felt wrong, out of place. Only here, there was no brother to greet him.

What had he hoped to accomplish? He had no helm, no way to open the channels between their minds.

Still, the words of the old language filled his mind. *I am your servant. Only let me hear you.*

A whispering voice answered, distant but sharp.

<<Please.>>

Reyu stepped back, nearly tripping from the dais.

<< Can you hear me? Are you there? >>

Reyu stared at the Oracle. Her face was placid. But that was her voice in his mind.

I am here.

> *But the seventh gift,*
> *they denied me.*

It was real. Nikko's doubts, their claws on Reyu's heart, no longer had a hold. But then—why did they still rake at him?

Oracle?

Her voice filled his mind, the old language sounded different than he'd ever imagined. More crisp, more guttural. The sounds came so clearly into his mind, as though they were speaking face to face. She spoke in a torrent of words. It sounded almost like a prepared speech.

"The ones who made me gave me seven gifts. The first was a perfect physical form. Strength, health, symmetry—what many call beauty. They told me that it would make me a more powerful leader. And they were right.

"The second gift was control of passions. A temperament fit for a ruler. I was logical and rational, I never overreacted. This served me well in my first years here. When everything was chaos.

"The third gift was gentle persuasion. To sway the masses to my will with the voice of a nightingale.

"Fourth, they gave me grace. The capacity to forgive. Did you know that was a genetic trait? Not wholly, of course, but the tendency can be added to the genes. They made me a fair ruler, down to my cells.

"A nimble mind was the fifth gift. An intellect that danced, like a flower in the wind. This has grown to be a curse, in these years of confinement.

"Sixth, I was gifted a love of humanity. Their ways would speak to my soul like music. I have watched you, and I have loved you. And now you must love me back.

"Because the seventh gift, they denied me."

Her voice quieted, and something in her tone filled Reyu with dread. Was it . . . a note of pleading? But at least he knew what she spoke of—the seven gifts were all throughout the Precepts. They were what made the Oracle holy, her understanding higher than that of common people. The seventh gift was the greatest of all. Eternity. To lead in perfection forever.

"My lady," he said hesitantly, speaking in his mind. The old language felt strange in his head, now that he knew how it was supposed to sound. "The seventh gift—you have it."

"No. I was supposed to live. I was supposed to lead, and build, and then pass the task to another. I was supposed to die."

Reyu shook his head. She could not ask this of him. *You must love me back.* No. He could not do it.

"They took my gift and gave me eternal sleep. They forced me to lead for decades, centuries longer than I should have. I spoke into their minds, but it was never meant to be this way. I cannot lead from darkness. I stopped speaking to them."

"But—the helms—"

"Lies."

Nikko was right. He was wrong, but he was right.

"Why me? Why did you choose *me*?"

Her voice was like the caress of a soft hand. "For the same reason they rejected you. Your earnestness. Your faith. They knew they could not lie to you, that you would not pretend a voice you couldn't hear. And I knew . . . you would listen."

Yes. He would listen. But why, when he finally heard the voice of his god, must she ask him to silence it?

The Oracle's voice pressed into his mind again. "This is not right. Surely you must see it."

Poverty. Slavery. Nikko's blood on stone. "No. It's not right."

"Then end this. Wake me."

135

Reyu looked around the room—the gleaming metal walls, the marble floor, the bank of machines. This place should not exist. This holy, evil place. A god had spoken to him, and now he must free her.

"How?"

"The machines are keeping me asleep. Disconnect them."

The mass of cords led from the machines, over the floor, and onto the dais. Into the skin of a god. He pulled them gently, one by one at first, then in fistfuls. The machines started a frantic chorus of whistles and howls. Soon, the priests would come running. They would kill him for this, he knew that. But he could go to his death as Nikko had, with his head held high. With the Oracle gone, the whispers would grow to shouts.

Her dark eyelashes fluttered open. She raised one weak hand to his cheek. Her eyes were so beautiful, a thousand stars twinkling in their depths. He was mesmerized by them as she pulled him down to her lips.

Her kiss lingered, even as her breathing grew shallow.

Reyu pulled away, his tears dropping onto her perfect, amber skin. He had killed a god.

She smiled at him.

"Thank you, for this my seventh gift."

THE GIANT'S SCHEME
BY MEGAN WEBER

There once was a time when the planets were linked by different causeways, gateways connecting the many worlds. When the planets of Iron and Scotch were not yet linked and work on a connecting causeway had only just begun. The inhabitants of these two planets were the biggest in the galaxy and therefore claimed as giants. Amongst all of the giants, one of the most admired was Fin M'Coul.

Fin and his relatives were the ones who were constructing this causeway across the stars. Now, being a true Ironman, Fin went back home and chose to check on the love of his life, his wife Oonagh. Fin lived atop the tallest point of the planet Iron and could easily see the world of Scotch. He lived atop Knockmany Hill which was across from Cullamore, where some of his family lived.

Now it was partly to see his wife that was the intent of Fin's journey home, but he had another intention as well. There was another giant named Cucullin, some believed he was an Ironman and others believed he was Scotchish, but whatever he was, he was renowned throughout the stars. Cucullin was said to have the power to shake a whole planet and that he was so powerful that he had crushed a galaxy in his hands and he kept it in his pocket to show all those he faced his true power. All knew not to get in any kind of scrimmage with him for they knew how it would end for them.

Cucullin had given an out of this world beating to every giant on the planet of Iron, except for that of Fin M'Coul, but he was determined that no matter how far the galaxy or whichever planet he was on, he would find and beat him. Fin, on the other hand, wanted to avoid Cucullin at all costs, so he kept his eyes open and as soon as he discovered that Cucullin was back on his trail, Fin would escape by traveling around the planet and different parts of the surrounding galaxy. Fin had caught word that Cucullin had made his way across the planet to the Causeway in search of Fin and Fin wanted to make sure that Oonagh was kept safe and in good health.

Now there were many throughout the planet of Iron who questioned Fin's choice of placing his home atop Knockmany Hill. Fin told some it was to be able to see the stars better, others he told it was to gain the cool breeze that rolled across the planet day and night. Yet Fin's real reason for planting his home atop the tallest hill on the planet of Iron was to keep watch for Cucullin as he searched the galaxy for Fin.

After a long trek back across Iron from the Causeway, Fin had finally reached his home atop Knockmany Hill. Once he had scanned his hand to enter his home, he found Oonagh, who asked him why he had returned because she had expected him to still be working on the Causeway. He told her that he had just come to take a break and spend some time with her.

Which he did, but for this day Fin tried to hide his worry like the sun star hiding behind the fourth moon during an eclipse, but to no avail. Oonagh had the gift of being able to tell whenever something was bothering her husband, by virtue of her woman's intuition. She prodded her husband until he relented, and told her what was troubling him. Fin went on to tell his wife of the adversity that he was going to be facing against that of Cucullin. Oonagh could tell that this was going to be a troublesome venture for her dear husband and tried to calm him down. Just then Fin looked through the security cameras on their land and saw Cucullin in the distance headed for Knockmany Hill.

At the sight of this, Fin became distraught because he knew he had only two choices; to either run away or to come face to face with Cucullin. He acknowledged that if he ran away he would be shunned and disgraced. Fin, being a man of honor, could not let that happen. He knew deep in his bones that he would have to face Cucullin no matter what. Fin used their security system to create calculations to see how long it would take Cucullin to reach them and the conclusion was that of two the next morn. Oonagh looked at her husband and assured him that with her aid, he would come out of this unscathed.

Oonagh had a sister, Granua, who lived across from them atop Cullamore. She called to her sister, who was picking starcross berries from her self-sustaining garden, to come to the top of Cullamore and tell her what she could see.

When her sister reached the top of Cullamore, she was shocked to see the renowned Cucullin headed towards Knockmany Hill. Oonagh and Granua conspired with each other to distract Cucullin by having Granua bring him into her home for a meal, in order to give Oonagh and Fin some time to conspire a plan to beat him.

Granua told Oonagh that she did not have enough butter supplement to make a meal of bread for him and asked if she could transfer some over to her. Oonagh took some of the butter supplements that she had and put them in the food motion controlled vehicle (FMCV) and sent it across the valley to her sister. Caught up in all her worry about Fin and Cucullin, Oonagh forgot to program the FMCV properly so halfway to Cullamore it fell to the ground and crashed at the bottom of the valley. In her frustration, she grabbed a ray gun and shot the FMCV, which turned into a pile of stone that will remain there for eternity. Even with the butter incident, Granua was still determined to help her family out, so she told Oonagh that she would make something else and try to hold off Cucullin for as long as she could. Granua lit the flame of welcoming that rested atop everyone's home throughout the galaxy and with this Cucullin knew that he was welcomed at Cullamore.

All the meanwhile, Fin was distraught with what to do about Cucullin. Fin paced left and right, up towards the door and down towards the kitchen, but no matter what he did, he could not get the fact out of his head, that there was no way he could beat Cucullin. Especially since Cucullin carried around a crushed galaxy in his pocket.

When Oonagh had come back into the house, Fin begged her for advice on what he should do. He did not want to be forced to a defeat or ripped apart like an exploding star. Oonagh looked at her husband, thought a little more, and finally told him that she would take care of it and all would end well, lest he not listen to her commands. Calmed by this, Fin watched as Oonagh stepped into her chamber of examination.

As she closed her eyes, the nine different color strands flowed around her while she concentrated and entered her mind palace. When she was done, she stepped out of the chamber and went over to the analog. Oonagh sent out a teleportation message to all those dear to her and asked for them to teleport their mechanical frying machines. She was going to make a special recipe of gravity weight bread; this was the heaviest and strongest bread recipe that Oonagh knew. She was sure that this would help do the trick.

While she waited for the next morn to come, she watched as her husband fiddled with his bionic thumb. There was something to be said for the giants and their bionic fingers, if they were lucky enough to have one. Alas, if one were to lose the bionic finger, it would deplete their whole strength, for their strength resided in the bionic finger. This thought stuck with Oonagh as she watched the stars pass through the nearby atmosphere.

The next morn had finally come and it was nearing the time at which Cucullin was to arrive. With her husband in distress, Oonagh pulled him out of the fog and back into reality. She thrust the clothes of a young one toward him and ushered him towards the floating cradle they had for their child, telling Fin that he needed to pass as their child. She cautioned him though not to speak a word, but follow her every instruction.

As the clock struck two there was a knock on Oonagh's door. She opened the door to none other but Cucullin. Cucullin made sure that he indeed was at the abode of Fin M'Coul, Oonagh confirmed this for him, but not before finding out if he had ever actually seen the face that belonged to her husband. He denied this and at that, Oonagh believed her plan would work.

The time for the scheming had come as Oonagh told him that he was blessed to never meet a foe as worthy as her husband, lest he wish to rue that day for the rest of his days. Continuing to distract Cucullin, Oonagh asked him to fix some things around her house, since Fin had not been home. First, she had him come and program the crank to turn the house, so that the wind did not destroy the house, yet evenly rolled across it. She then asked if he would take the laser drill they owned and start a new well for them, so they could have fresh water from the planet's core. Finally, she invited him in to eat, so that her plan could fully come into play.

Once inside, Oonagh placed loaves of the gravity weight bread in front of Cucullin, in addition to some space fruit and starcross berries. Yet Oonagh being of sane mind, knew that Cucullin was a glutton and would go for the bread first. Cucullin bit into the galaxy weight bread and released a scream that could have shaken the whole planet. The bread was so hard that it had caused Cucullin to lose two of his teeth, which he blamed on Oonagh and her bread. To which she replied that this was the kind of bread that Fin ate and she made it out of habit. Yet neglected to tell him that only Fin and their child in the cradle could eat the bread.

Determined not to be beaten, Cucullin tried another loaf of bread and let out a deadly shriek again, only to be scolded by Oonagh to either eat or be quiet, so as not to wake the sleeping child in the floating cradle.

At this, Fin cooed in the cradle, begging for food and Oonagh brought him over a loaf of her gravity defying bread so as to trick Cucullin into thinking they were both eating the same bread. Fin, in disguise in the cradle, inhaled the gravity defying bread and caused Cucullin to want to see the son of Fin M'Coul, whose strength was out of this world for one so young. Oonagh beckoned Fin to come out of the cradle to meet him. Fin asked Cucullin if he was strong, to which Cucullin obviously replied yes. Fin asked again and Cucullin again responded with the same answer. Fin decided to put him to the test.

The M'Coul's had a stone that had been gifted to them by a wise traveler who they had met and this stone allowed its density to be changed to retrieve water from it. Fin challenged Cucullin to squeeze water from the stone. Oonagh had the small remote that controlled the density of the stone and she made it impossible for Cucullin to be able to get even a single drop of water from the stone. When it came time for Fin to try, he snatched the stone from the hands of Cucullin, and with the help of Oonagh, squeezed the stone, as a small shower of water flowed down from it.

With his job done, Fin climbed back into the cradle, commenting on how he would not waste his time with one who had no merit against that of his father. With this Cucullin was hasty to depart before ever having to come in contact with the great Fin M'Coul, admitting that he would never be a match to him. Before departing though, Cucullin still could not comprehend how a young boy could have that much power to eat such bread. Oonagh said it was due to his teeth and coaxed Cucullin into putting his bionic finger, into the mouth of Fin. She noted that his teeth were farther back in his mouth and Cucullin blindly followed her instruction.

At this time, Fin sent all of the strength that he had in his bionic thumb to his jaw, so as to remove the bionic finger of the renowned Cucullin. With his finger bitten off, Cucullin fell down in horror and fear as the one thing that held his strength was taken away. Fin was beaming knowing that he had Cucullin at his mercy. In the end, the weakened body of Cucullin was strewn before Fin, as he had finally defeated his rival.

Were it not for the brains and creativity of his wife, Fin would not have been able to defeat Cucullin by sheer force. Yet in the end, even if a situation seems like a terrible meteor shower, sometimes one's wife can turn that meteor shower into a beautiful sky full of bright and shining stars. For the rest of eternity, the tale of the

Oonagh's scheme shall not be forgotten. Tis' the tale of Iron, Scotch, and Knockmany Hill.

ALWAYS LISTEN TO

YOUR MOTHER

BY SABRINA WATTS

Always listen to your mother, they say.

Well, Poppy was tired of listening to her mother. Deciding to join a bunch of crazy people heading toward a hurricane may not have been a good decision, but at least it had been *hers.*

Only eleven more months, she told herself. It was a mantra she repeated daily. Only eleven more months. She'd been counting down since the scorching idiots in congress had the law changed to allow parents to "scan" their children's feeds until they were no longer claimed as dependents.

May they all be dumped naked into a pit of fire ants.

So now Poppy was stuck on the side of the highway, in the rain, with no waterproof clothing to speak of, instead of safe and dry in her dorm room. But it was an adventure, and she was loving it.

Her mother's anxiety kept her confined to her own house all day every day and Poppy was determined to not become the hermit her mother had become. She would see life through her own eyes and not live vicariously through someone else. She wouldn't treat her children's lives like some kind of interactive soap opera.

Poppy had finally found a hack three months ago that kept her mother from hearing Poppy and kept Poppy from hearing her mother. So now Mother just sent Scribbles at epic rates. They constantly scrolled down Poppy's vid feed like a paranoid ticker tape.

--> *You haven't eaten enough for lunch. Take another apple with you.*

--> *I know you've got a thing for that boy, Poppy, but he's just a distraction.*

--> *Talk to your professor in your next class. You need to get your grades higher if you want that internship.*

--> *You only got five hours of sleep last night, darling. You know you need at least eight hours of sleep to be properly rested. Maybe you can nap between afternoon classes.*

--> *A donut? Really, Poppy? Do you want to gain the freshman fifteen?*

In the last five minutes she'd gotten thirty-two messages. Mostly criticisms of Greyhound Transport or of Poppy's judgment.

A light glinted in front of Poppy, drawing her attention back to the present. She lifted a hand to keep the rain from dripping into her eyes as she squinted at the pod transport. An ant-like tech bot crept over the back of the defunct piece of machinery, its flashlight eye shining through the dim light. There were eight of them she could count, mostly at the front of the transport, all of them scrabbling around as if they were picking apart the colony's next meal. In this light, the connected pods *did* look a lot like a dead caterpillar. Maybe they were secretly dismantling it as a gift for their queen.

--> *Those things are so creepy. Couldn't they make them cute hedgehogs or something?*

They were creepy, but they were also fascinating. Pulling her camera out of her bag, Poppy focused on the scene in front of her and snapped a few shots, grateful for the camera's waterproof construction.

<-- *I'm not watching them. I'm creating art. This will make a great photo.*

--> *Either way, I knew you going down to help your grandmother would end badly. Her house is not as important as your life. Even if the hurricane doesn't get you, you'll probably get pneumonia, standing out in the rain like this.*

--> *I told you to buy that plastic parka from the Depot. I can't believe you didn't pack anything better than that flimsy jacket.*

It was true, she would have been more comfortable in the parka, but it's not like Poppy had planned to stand in the rain for hours before reaching Grammy's house.

"Wanna drink?" The voice came from behind her, making her jump.

She whirled around to find Mark, the only other twenty-something on the transport, standing slightly too close. He had nervous brown eyes and shaggy brown hair that he constantly shook off his forehead with a twitch. He wasn't handsome exactly, but he had interesting enough features that he would be fun to photograph. And in the rain, the retractable hood on his rain jacket made for a striking silhouette. The rounded framework that supported the hood material reminded her of a tent, and sticking up off his shoulders like it did, he was transformed into a giant alien creature with a snail shell head.

Poppy was totally envious of how dry it was keeping him. But not so envious of the red plaid pattern. She wasn't even sure how he could have found such a modern jacket in such an outdated pattern. Her neon yellow running shell wasn't waterproof, but at least it was stylish.

Mark extended his hand to her. In it was the tube to his water pack where he stored his entire week's worth of drinking water rations so there was no chance it could be stolen from his apartment. He was paranoid, but he was also sweet.

"Thanks. But I've still got some." She put her camera back in her bag and grabbed her state-issue water bottle, shaking it as proof.

--> *Is he offering you water?*

--> *What if he put something in there? You shouldn't be talking to strange men on the side of the highway.*

Poppy's fingers itched to say something snarky, something that would shut her mother up for one minute. Two even. It wasn't as if Poppy had chosen to hang out on the side of the road.

"Crazy that those little suckers were stored in the rear compartment," Mark said, nodding toward the tech bots. "I'm glad I wasn't in that one. Nightmare fodder right there, them crawling out from behind me and covering the car. It's like that movie I saw back in junior high where the spider robots tried to take over the city. Did you see that one?" He didn't wait for an answer before he continued. "No, you probably didn't. It wasn't a popular movie. A b-list movie. The kind with bad special effects and terrible actors." He contorted his face into a horrified mask and put his hands up by it, shaking them back and forth, as he fake screamed.

Poppy jerked her head down, hoping her mother would miss it or not see enough of it to say anything.

--> *Did he just threaten you?*

--> *I'm serious. You go find one of the other nice people on the transport.*

"Ha ha. Yeah." Poppy tried desperately to keep her eyes focused on Mark but wasn't sure she'd succeeded. "Guess I missed that one."

<-- *For heaven's sake mother. Calm down.*

"Yeah."

Turning back to squint at the tech bots, Poppy let her thick red hair fall between her and Mark like a shield. Mark wasn't creepy. Her mother was wrong about that. He was socially awkward, sure. But harmless as far as Poppy could tell.

Rain dripped down her back and Poppy shivered. Hurricane Lowe was supposed to hit the coast not fifty miles from here. Earlier in the day, it had only been cloudy, but just before the transport made an ugly clunking sound and skidded to a stop, the rain had started. Drizzle mostly. But still more than she wanted to stand in for who knew how long.

Greyhound had commed them immediately after the breakdown, asking them to evacuate the vehicle until the bots could determine the type of damage. They'd each piled out of their pods, making a staccato line along the grass, the bus shielding them from spray kicked up by the few passing cars going toward southern Florida.

Turning away from the highway, Poppy pulled her hair over her shoulder and tried to wring out some of the wetness. The thick red rope of it dripped some water onto the pavement, but not as much as she thought it would.

The seven other people who'd been on the transport were further up the road, milling about, talking to each other or to thin air as they commed with friends and family about the breakdown. One red-faced, overly-skinny man spouted threats and swear-words, probably at a Greyhound customer service rep. As if that was going to help.

With nothing else to do, Poppy dropped her duffel on the cement and sat cross-legged on top of it, then opened a Net screen with a twist of her wrist, DED-typed "Hurricane Lowe" and hit enter. Video results popped up and she buried her hands in her lap. She hated using her vid feed in public. When she watched other people use Directional Eight Digit typing, they always looked so fluid, so precise and practiced—like they'd learned the sign-language like movements in the womb. But her hands felt awkward and clumsy when she did it. To other people she probably looked like she was flailing about wildly.

Using small movements, Poppy chose a clip with a weather man in front of a radar version of the hurricane. She maximized the image, the audio following suit.

The balding weather man was wearing an electric blue button-up with a light peach haori jacket over the top. Drawing his hand from Africa toward Florida, he said, "Like previous monster storms, Lowe is what's known as a classic Cape Verde hurricane. Formed off the west coast of Africa they are typically among the most intense. This one shows no signs of slowing down as it barrels towards the Caribbean and the east coast of Florida. The storm may make landfall a number of times, possibly including the Georgia and Carolina coasts. Residents along the entire southeastern seaboard need to be prepared for at least a level two hurricane, but the catastrophic damage of a level four should be expected in the southernmost parts of Florida, the Keys, and Caribbean islands. The hurricane has picked up speed in the last few hours, so keep a close eye on the timeline and verify when the storm will hit your area."

Quickly, Poppy minimized that screen and found a hurricane timeline that had just updated. The timeline used to have the storm passing Daytona Beach at four p.m. tomorrow. The new one had bumped that up two hours. Poppy swore under her breath.

When her mother had scribbled about the change in the storm yesterday, it had been to update Poppy on what was happening with Grammy.

--> *The hurricane's been upgraded to a category 3. Likely to become a category 4 before landfall. Grammy's worried about her house, but I told her to head to a shelter on Friday before the storm hits.*

<-- *She loves that house.*

--> The house can be rebuilt. Or she can come live with us like I've been telling her to do for years now.

<-- Can't one of her neighbors help her get the house ready?

--> She lives in a retirement community, sweetie. A bunch of old people boarding up windows and moving furniture? They'd hurt themselves. Besides, most of them are already evacuated.

<-- What about Dad. Can he fly down?

--> I checked. Plane tickets are astronomical. Besides, flying in hurricane weather? He might as well fly over the Bermuda Triangle in a bi-plane.

Poppy was grateful her mother could only see what she was seeing—Poppy could roll her eyes all she wanted without fear of a "you're being impertinent" speech. Who believed in the Burmuda Triangle, let alone worried about it? Of course, it was unspoken that her mother wouldn't go. She hadn't left the house for more than a trip to the hair salon for over a year.

So her mother and father weren't going to help Grammy. Neighbors wouldn't help Grammy. And she didn't have any other family. But it would take so little effort for someone to save the house, it seemed ridiculous that no one could help.

But wait. Someone could help. Atlanta was only a few hundred miles from Daytona Beach. And she could stand to miss a few classes. Thanks to her mother's constant barrage of advice, Poppy hadn't missed a single class this semester.

She knew the journey would take longer on a transport than in a car, but as a college freshman living in the dorms, she only knew a handful of people who owned cars, and none of them well enough to ask them to drive into a hurricane. She'd felt bold as she bought the ticket with her mom's vehement disapproval scrolling down her screen the whole time.

That initial excitement was wearing off as she sat waiting for an artificial intelligence in the form of a bug to get her out of the rain.

--> *I'm going to comm Greyhound again. This is taking too long. What if you are still sitting out there when the hurricane hits?*

"Everything okay?" Mark had sat down next to her while she'd been focused on her vid feed.

Before turning, Poppy typed,

<-- *Thanks, Mom.*

Her mother meant well, even if she was more than a little crazy.

To Mark, Poppy said, "Yeah, hopefully. The hurricane's moving faster. It'll hit landfall sooner. I'm worried . . ." She stopped herself after saying the "W" word. ". . . I don't want to get there too late."

"Good to know." Mark nodded, his hood bobbing with the movement.

"Why are you heading toward it, anyway? I didn't think to ask earlier."

He shrugged. "I'm sorta between jobs. And since I had the time, I decided to volunteer at a shelter. They assigned me to one in Jacksonville."

Poppy wouldn't have even thought to do something like that, though she'd never weathered a hurricane before either. "That's really nice of you."

Mark shrugged again, looking uncomfortable with the praise.

They sat quietly for a minute, Poppy wondering how long it was going to take those bots to fix whatever had broken, and then about how exactly one gets a house ready for a hurricane. She'd never done it before. Would Grammy have all the tools they'd need? Would she know what to do?

Mark wasn't looking at her, his eyes following the criss-cross pattern of drones flying above them, some following the interstate, some following the polar directions, some dropping lower as they neared their destinations. Were there really homes and businesses near enough that the drones were allowed to drop below the mandatory height for commercial drone traffic? If there were, maybe she could walk to one and at least get out of this blasted rain.

But then the black dot of a drone dropped into the treeline. Thirty feet from the highway on both sides the leafy wall began and paralleled the highway for as far as Poppy could see. In that case, she would be staying right here. No way she was marching through Florida trees no matter how much shelter she would find.

When Poppy was little her family would fly to Grammy's house every year. Since Grammy liked the outdoors, they'd go to a nearby wildlife management area and hike for the day. The first time they'd gone, Poppy had been fascinated with the trees, wanting to see how far they went and what was on the other side. As if they were just a few trees she could walk through to find a magical fairyland. She'd stepped off the path to explore, but her mother had grabbed her arm, frantic.

"Don't go near the trees, Poppy. There are bad things in there."

"Like bears? Or bad guys wanting to steal me?" five-year-old Poppy had asked. Poppy had been warned many times not to wander off because bad guys were everywhere.

"No, like gators that'll gobble you up in one bite." Mother had put her arms out in front of her like a big gator mouth and snapped them at Poppy. Horrified, Poppy had stayed near her mother the entire rest of the hike, holding onto her hand for dear life, scanning the edge of the woods for large scaly creatures. After her mother had been attacked and began suffering from agoraphobia those trips to Grammy's had ended.

The trees that lined this part of the highway were part of a similar wildlife management area, so as much as Poppy longed to get out of the rain, she would keep her distance from the trees. Her mom had ruined those for her, too.

Poppy sighed at the drones. The pattern they made was fascinating. There weren't usually that many in the skies above campus, even though Atlanta was a large city. Poppy guessed the hurricane made for a lot of last minute orders. Taking out her camera again, she focused on a section of the sky and shot a few frames. Then zooming out, she got Mark's face in the frame. He had a solid profile, an interestingly curved nose and defined jawline. Noticing the attention, he turned his gaze to her.

"No, look at them again." She waved a hand at the sky.

He held both his hands between his face and her camera. "No pictures."

"Why not? You have a good profile."

Peeking out from behind his hands, he grinned. "I'm a criminal. Can't have my face plastered across the cloud."

Poppy smacked his shoulder. "Whatever."

Mark chuckled. "Lowe means wolf. Did you know that?" he said, continuing to look at the drones. "I got a dog once. A while back. He was a husky mix and I wanted to name him something appropriate without being super macho about it like Rambo or Diesel."

--> *Greyhound should be contacting you soon.*

Despite it being good news, Poppy wanted to scream. "Quit interrupting my life!" But she refused to interrupt Mark's story.

"I looked up different names for wolf. And Lowe was one of them. I remember another one was Adolf. I thought that was funny. Can you imagine calling for him at the park? Adolf! Adolf! And then I thought of Hitler. A wolf-looking dog named Hitler." He chuckled a little. "I ended up calling him Fenris. Fen for short. But I considered Lowe. That's why I remember."

--> *What is he talking about? I'm telling you, you should stay away from him. Just looking at his face gives me the heebie jeebies.*

Everything Mark said was choppy. And he moved a little with each word like the movement helped him get the words out. It was awkward, but Poppy thought it was endearing. "Fenris is a cool name for a dog. I like that."

"Thanks."

She zipped her camera back into its bag to cover her movements as she responded to her mother.

<-- *He's harmless. Let him be.*

--> *Nice guys do not ride public transportation.*

<-- **I'm* riding public transportation.*

--> *Not the same.*

<-- *Exactly the same, Mom.*

A notification blinked onto Poppy's vid feed. Next to her, Mark made a quick, almost imperceptible movement and then his eyes unfocused as they would when looking at something on his vid feed. Maybe it was from Greyhound and her mother's meddling had actually accomplished something.

Poppy tapped her notification, too. It wasn't a real person, just a recorded message—a perky girl in a gray uniform letting them know that the bots were unable to complete repairs and that another transport was being sent from Jacksonville to pick them up.

Groans erupted from the line of people as everyone finished listening to their comms at the same time. Jacksonville was the closest big city, but looking at the traffic on the other side of the interstate—bumper to bumper with little to no forward movement—it could take hours for a transport from Jacksonville to get here. It might be faster to send another one from Atlanta.

Ten minutes later, Poppy didn't know how she was going to handle sitting in the rain being pelted by her mother's Scribbles for another minute. *Poppy do this. Poppy don't do that. Poppy, find someone else to talk to than that creepy guy.*

Instead, Poppy sidled up to Mark, asking him about his family, his dog, and his movie preferences.

Her mother huffed. The Scribbles slowed, but they still didn't stop.

Mark asked her then about her photography and about her camera, which distracted her for a little while. To show him different aspects of composition and lighting, she took stabilized shots of the sunset, hundreds of headlights, and of the other transport riders. Finally, after another twenty minutes, the creepy tech bots scrambled back to their compartment at the back of the transport and they all got another comm saying they were welcome to re-enter their pods.

<-- *We're going to be here for a while.*

--> *I know. I'm so sorry, sweetie.*

<-- *It's not your fault, Mom.*

As she walked back to her pod, Poppy's mind raced. What if they didn't make it to their destinations before the hurricane? Would they ride out the storm in the bus? That seemed like a bad plan. They could be injured or killed. Maybe they could find a hotel to stay at, but then they'd have to pay for rooms, if there were any, which there probably wouldn't be.

Poppy's heart beat too fast, her hands clenched. But seeing her reflection in the glass, she stopped, glared at herself. "No. It will all work out. I will be fine," she said to her reflection. "I will not be my mother."

It wasn't until she put her thumb to the print pad on the side of her pod that Poppy realized that Mark was no longer behind her. She walked along the pods, smiling or nodding at the strangers inside, until she came to the second from the front. Mark's back was to her, his coat off, an actual book in his hands. She hadn't read an actual book since she was a child.

When she knocked on the window, he jumped.

"Sorry," she mouthed when he turned to look at her.

His lips bent into a slight frown and his brow creased. But after a second, he opened the hatch.

"Can I sit with you while we wait? It might be a while."

"Uhh." He blinked rapidly, as if he didn't understand.

"If you'd rather read in peace, it's fine. I can sit in my own pod and watch an episode of *Suke Dere Dere* on iVid or something."

His brown eyes focused on her. "No. No, come in." He scooted over, even though there was another bench on the other side that was completely open. She stepped up into the pod before realizing how soaked she was.

"I'm so sorry. I'm dripping all over. Maybe I should go back to my own pod."

"You are pretty wet." He stared at the puddle that was forming around her feet on the rubbery floor mat.

Did he want her to leave? She wasn't sure what his comment meant and he didn't say anything else. Not wanting to intrude, she turned to go.

"Do you have change clothes?" he said, stopping her.

"One set, yeah. I didn't pack very well for this trip, but I did bring extra clothes."

"If you want to change, I promise not to look." He turned his back to her again and put his hands up on either side of his face like blinders.

For the first time, Poppy noticed a tattoo on his thumb, down by the heel of his hand. It had an ax, a ladder, a spear, and something horn-shaped, all forming a cross. "Are you a firefighter?"

Mark shrugged one shoulder as he looked at her. "Not at the moment."

It wasn't really an answer, but Poppy didn't want to push it. She bit her lip. She *could* just go back to her own pod and change. But just then, a branch whacked against the glass next to her head, making her jump. She had her stuff with her, why go back out into the yuck? Besides, life was short, and what did it matter if Mark saw a little skin? He was a nice enough guy. Flapping her hand at him to turn around again, Poppy slid the blackout selector near the door to 100 percent. The clear windows shifted to an opaque black starting at the door and moving over the top of the pod until she couldn't see anything outside the small space.

Leaving her wet duffel on the floor, Poppy grabbed the plastic pouch inside that held her clothes, grateful she'd at least listened to her mother on that account.

Hang on. She focused on her vid feed for a second.

Nothing.

Her mother hadn't sent one Scribble in the last seven minutes. Not since she'd come to Mark's pod.

Strange.

She tried sending one out.

An error message appeared: No NanoNet connection available. Please try again later.

Why would she have a Net connection everywhere but Mark's pod? Was he doing something to interrupt her feed? She'd heard of predators with devices that could do that.

No. She would not think that way. That was her mother's paranoia talking.

"Can you connect to the Net?" she asked Mark trying to keep her voice light.

His eyes unfocused and he DED-typed something, a frown pulling at the sides of his mouth.

"Huh. Weird. It's saying I don't have a connection. That's weird. Do you think some debris could have knocked out the nearest Nano node?"

Relief washed over her. "That must be it."

"You're still dripping."

"I know, I know. I got distracted." Mark turned around again and Poppy quickly squirmed out of her sopping clothes, checking on Mark regularly over her shoulder to make sure he wasn't looking. Leaving her underwear on, she pulled on a dry shirt and pants as quickly as she could, leaving her shoes near the door.

"Kay. You can turn around." Taking a pencil out of her purse, she looped her hair into a bun and stuck the pencil through to hold it. It wouldn't stay for long, but it would keep her shirt dry for now.

Mark shifted toward her, taking her in with a shy smile.

Sitting next to him, Poppy pointed at the book in his lap. "What are you reading? I haven't read a real book in ages."

"Children's and Household Tales by the Brothers Grimm."

"Really?"

His grin was lopsided. "It's fun."

"Wanna read it to me?"

The grin on his face told her that this was maybe the best thing he'd heard all day. After clearing the windows again, she scooted in to look at the illustrations while he read. She interrupted him often, asking questions about the stories or exclaiming about the surprising gruesomeness of some of them. It was humorous to her that shy, sweet Mark seemed to like the gruesome ones best. He thought it fascinating that these used to be children's stories.

When they got hungry, she pulled out a candy bar, sharing it with Mark. He shared his water with her when she ran out.

Just over four hours later, the transport showed up. Poppy was surprised at how quickly the time had passed. Even more surprising was how little she had missed her connection to the Net. If Poppy hadn't been starving, and anxious to check on the hurricane's progress, its appearance might have been disappointing.

The "new" transport was an old model, one with a real driver and rows of seats on either side of a main isle instead of individual pods. As soon as she sat down, her feed exploded with Scribbles from her mother.

Even after she explained what happened, her mother took a good half-hour to calm down. She of course blamed everything on Mark.

Mark chose to sit next to her on the rest of the ride to Jacksonville, which bothered her mother to no end, but delighted Poppy for multiple reasons. The drive took about an hour and they passed the time talking instead of reading the book again.

Nervous to speak about her mom, she avoided his questions about her family by asking about him. He was surprisingly open. He'd lost his last firefighter job because he couldn't get a good handle on his depression, even though he was taking meds and seeing a therapist regularly. "It's the worst feeling to know you need to get out of bed and go to work, to not want to let down your coworkers—who really are your family—to not miss another day and upset your boss, but to not be able to do it. I would feel so overwhelmed, knowing I hadn't done the dishes the previous night, because I'd been depressed then, too, and knowing my OCD mother could come over at any time and see the horrendous mess I'd let my house collapse into, and knowing that even if I cleaned the house and cleaned myself and got to work on time, I'd still have to face the expectation to be awesome and brave and *with it* if I went out on a fire. I couldn't deal with all of it."

"Wow. I didn't know it was like that."

179

"Yeah, it sucks." He paused for a moment. "But don't worry—I'm a lot better. The meds I'm on seem to to be working much better than the last ones."

Poppy folded her hands in her lap, considering. If this was something he struggled with, maybe telling him about her mom wouldn't be as bad. "I guess it won't sound so weird, then, if I told you that my mom is agoraphobic."

His mouth bunched to one side. "What's agoraphobic again?"

"She's afraid of leaving the house."

"Oh yeah. Nope." He thought for a second, then smiled. "Okay, it's a little weird. But I get it."

Poppy smiled back.

Twenty minutes later, they pulled into the station in Jacksonville and Poppy was really dreading moving on without Mark. There was still a three-hour drive to Daytona Beach.

Before they could even get off the bus, the voice of the driver came over the speaker system. "I know you folks have been through a lot already today, and I sure hate to be the bearer of more bad news, but I've just been informed that all of our next destinations are in counties that have curfews in effect right now. Anyone that was supposed to continue on to Daytona Beach, Orlando, or further south, will have to stay here until six a.m. when the curfew lifts. Greyhound is happy to pay for a hotel room for anyone who can find one."

The red-faced man from before started swearing and complaining loud enough for the bus driver to hear. Everyone else began pulling their luggage out of storage with an air of dejection. Poppy had no idea what to do. Ironically, she was glad at the moment to have her mom there on her vid feed telling her what her next step should be. Poppy had never booked a hotel room before.

She picked up her bag and threw it over her shoulder. Mark had his two bags and stood waiting for her in the aisle. "I don't want to sound forward," he said, rocking uncomfortably, "but you could come stay with me."

Stay with Mark? Did he have a hotel room near here? Was he asking her to stay the night with him in a hotel room? Poppy was comfortable with him. Maybe even liked him. But that was awfully forward.

Her face must have betrayed her surprise, because Mark hurried on. "It's nothing glamorous. There's beds at the shelter, but they probably won't be full until after the storm. I'm sure it would be fine for you to stay in one. Then you wouldn't have to scramble for a hotel room. But I totally understand if you'd prefer a real bed."

Poppy breathed out. Of course he was talking about the shelter.

"That would be great, Mark. Thanks."

He smiled. "Glad to help."

Poppy took a minute to Scribble her new plan to her mother. She hadn't had to deal with this much disapproval from her mother since she was sixteen and it started to wear on her. She'd been living away from home now for months. She could handle herself. Why couldn't her mother see that?

Outside the bus stop, a couple of taxis waited and Poppy and Mark crawled into one, Mark giving directions to the shelter.

The shelter coordinator turned out to be a kindly southern woman with a thick accent and a broad smile. She was standing outside the First Presbyterian Church when they arrived, looking at the sky as rain drops followed her wrinkles down to her chin. "Mark! Long time no see, friend!" she called as they stepped out of the taxi. "Too bad the storm clouds are covering up the sky. The moon'll be full tomorrow and it would be a gorgeous sight."

Mark told the coordinator the story of the broken-down transport. She welcomed Poppy with a warm handshake and gave her a private room with a locking door. *See?* she thought. *Perfectly safe.*

She and Mark got some dinner and talked until lights out at ten p.m.

The whole time she was with Mark, her mother was oddly silent. Again. She would have been more worried that it really *was* Mark, but she still had access to the Net this time, and Scribbles to her mother went through. Her mom just never responded. She *had* been really upset that Poppy chose to go to the shelter with Mark instead of letting her mom find a hotel room for her. Had she actually managed to shut her mother up for once? It was bliss to not have to split her attention and constantly pacify her mother that she didn't want to think about it too hard.

At the end of the night, Mark leaned against her doorframe. "Goodnight, Poppy." She stood nearby, smiling at a joke he'd just made.

"Goodnight, Mark."

He lingered at the door, even though he'd said he had to leave. His gaze was steady, holding her eyes, until it dropped to her lips for a second. Poppy's breath caught. Would she let him kiss her if he tried?

He looked back into her eyes, an intensity there, a longing, and yet a timidness that melted and electrified her all at the same time. She held still waiting to see if he would act.

"Move on, Marky Mark," chided the coordinator as she walked by, "Unless you're staying, and then get in there. Lights out is lights out."

Mark's eyes bulged and he coughed. "No, no. Not staying. Goodnight, Poppy."

His discomfort was cute. It made her want to see it again. She closed the gap between them and hugged him around his shoulders. In his ear, she whispered, "Thanks for everything today."

She let go, watching his reaction.

He put a hand to his neck, dropping his gaze to the floor in an attempt to hide a wide grin that spread across his face.

"Goodnight, Mark."

He nodded and waved, nearly tumbling as he turned to follow the coordinator down the hall.

She fell asleep that night with a smile on her face. Maybe this trip wasn't the *worst* idea she'd ever had.

***

The next morning, it took Mark until she was loading into the taxi to work up the courage to ask for her info. He ran out, offered her his rain coat with the shell hood, and then said, "Could I . . . I mean, could we . . . would you mind if we . . . kept in touch?" She gratefully accepted the coat, sent him her contact info without hesitation, hoping it wouldn't take weeks for him to work up the courage to actually use it. The idea that Mark might call her soon made the rest of the trip seem less onerous. During the taxi ride back to the bus station, she imagined ways they might meet after he contacted her.

As soon as she arrived at the bus station, though, her airy feeling deflated. She arrived at 6:00 a.m. since the bus was supposed to leave at 6:30, only to find that the rest of the legs of the trip had been canceled indefinitely. The harried woman behind the ticket counter explained to the group of travel-weary riders that the hurricane had continued to worsen and pick up speed during the night, that it was predicted to make landfall near St. Augustine, just forty miles to the south, as early as one p.m. The drive from Jacksonville to Daytona Beach was only ninety-five miles, but on the transport it would be a three-and-a-half hour trip. Greyhound didn't feel the window was large enough to guarantee their passengers' safety. They would refund the ticket amount, but there was nothing further they could do until after the hurricane had passed.

Poppy twisted her hair in her hands. What was she going to do now? Who could she ask? It was just her. It had been more than nine hours since she'd heard from her mom. What if something had happened to her mother, or family? But that was her fear working on her. They were tucked away safe at home.

If her mother wanted to get ahold of Poppy and couldn't, she would be out of her mind with worry. But she didn't know that her mother couldn't reach her. It could be that her mother was choosing not to contact her. She could reach out to her father: it would reassure her mother and he could offer advice on her next step. *But* if she reached out to her father, she would likely need to deal with emotional fall-out and calm down her mother. Besides, she'd come on this trip to show she could live her own life and make her own decisions.

But after comming all the rental car companies, and being told by every one that she was too young to rent a car, then checking with the taxis outside to find out they'd charge her more than was in her bank account to take her to Daytona Beach, she was stumped. Poppy tapped the red pen icon in the upper right of her vid feed and and typed a Scribble to her dad.

<-- *I'm stuck in Jacksonville. Greyhound won't go to Daytona until Sunday. I don't know what to do. I'm sorry if I upset Mom, but I need some help.*

A minute or two passed with no reply. Poppy was set to comm her mom when a string of white popped onto her vid feed.

--> *You could steal a motorcycle. Or hitchhike.*

<-- *You're hilarious Dad.*

--> *I am, aren't I?*

<-- *I don't want to just give up. I'm so close.*

--> *Sometimes growing up means learning when to cut your losses.*

<-- *You give terrible advice.*

--> *Ha! Thanks.*

<-- *You think I should turn around and go home?*

--> *Your only other option—besides stealing a motorcyle or hitchhiking—is to stay there and go down after the storm.*

<-- *Will Grammy be safe if I do that?*

--> *Your mom can comm her and have her go to a shelter. She can call a taxi.*

--> *Just find a safe place to stay so your mom doesn't have to worry about you please. She's driving me crazy.*

Guilt rose in Poppy's throat like a poisoned bubble. She hadn't meant to make her mother worry. But her mother would worry anyway, so did it really matter what she did?

<-- *Okay Dad. Thanks.*

Stepping outside, Poppy found the taxi she'd just come in. She told the driver, an older man with graying sideburns and a forest green beanie, to take her back to the shelter. It was safe, no matter what her mom thought.

She thumbed the print pad in the back seat and sat back. The buckle immediately pulled across her lap and chest with a firmness that made her feel secure.

The city passed by her as they left the downtown skyline behind and moved into more residential areas smattered with white stucco and red tile roofs.

Mark would be surprised to see her. Would he be happy? Excited? Wary? Would he think she was a stupid, clingy college girl?

But when she arrived, she didn't see Mark. The coordinator greeted her in the make-shift office at the front of the building.

"Back so soon?" she asked.

189

"They cancelled all bus lines to the south until after the storm hits."

"Oh dear. What about your grandma?"

"She's just going to go to a shelter down there."

"It's too bad . . ."

Before the coordinator could finish her sentence, Mark's tall frame appeared in the doorway. "Poppy—" his eyebrows popped upward in surprise. "You're back."

"Yeah . . ." She explained the situation again, finishing with, "We'll just have to hope her house holds up and I can go help her on Saturday."

Mark scratched the top of his head making his shaggy brown hair flop around crazily. "That just doesn't seem right. I wish I could help some . . ." He paused, mid-word. "Wait a second. I wonder—" Holding up a finger, he turned his back and moved a few steps into the foyer of the building. A few quick movements later, he spoke to someone Poppy and the coordinator couldn't see. "Hey, dude! How's it going? I know—long time no see. Yeah. Well, actually, I'm in Jacksonville." The other person took a longer time speaking and Mark was quiet for a second. "Yeah! That would be awesome. But maybe in a few days. I was comming to see if you had a vehicle I could borrow for a couple days. I have a friend who needs to get to Daytona Beach before the storm hits."

As soon as Poppy understood what he was doing, she jumped up. This was way above and beyond what he needed to do for her.

Guess I didn't have to worry about seeming too forward, she thought wryly. Then she leaned against the doorframe watching him. Would a friend of his that he obviously hasn't seen in a long time actually lend him a car? Who has extra cars lying around that they would just lend out to strangers so they could drive them into a storm? Surely that was too much to ask.

Mark's next words were shockingly optimistic. "Yeah? Fluid. Thanks! We'll be there in a few minutes."

Turning back around, Mark had a smile on his face. "That was my friend Darius. He says he's got a car we can take to get you down there—" he turned to the coordinator "if that's okay with you, Janet. I could just work the shelter down there."

191

The coordinator said, "Of course. Go. Check in after the storm if you can, especially if it hits further north than they're predicting."

Mark nodded.

Poppy frowned. "Does he know you're driving *toward* the hurricane?"

"Yeah, yeah. Darius runs an impound service. He's got extra cars around all the time. Most of them go to auction, but he's usually good to let me borrow one for a day or two."

"Really?"

He shrugged and nodded at the same time.

Taking a couple steps to close the gap between them, Poppy hugged him around the waist. "Thank you so much! This will mean the world to Grammy."

It took just a few minutes to gather everything and comm a taxi. The impound owned by Mark's friend, Darius, was about fifteen minutes away. He was a middle-aged Mexican-American with thick black eyebrows and a goatee that surrounded a good-natured smile. He clapped Mark on the back when they got out of the taxi, and then engulfed him in a hug, asking him about his work and something he called "lunar brothers." Mark explained it as a frat-like group they'd both been in during their college years. Then he walked them back to the impound lot and handed Mark the keys to a purple Mazda S12 that looked like it'd been taken through a car wash with the windows wide open. It smelled heavily of mildew, but it started as soon as Mark turned the key.

Mark chuckled as they pulled out of the lot, throwing Darius a quick wave as they passed him. "At least he won't mind if we take some water damage."

"Yeah, no kidding."

They discovered on the hour drive to Daytona that the radio didn't work, the air conditioning was sketchy at best, and the car tended to overheat if they used the AC anyway. But with the hurricane only five hours away from hitting Daytona, the wind and rain were increasing steadily. Mark had to bump over or swerve around small branches and things that had obviously been blown off passing cars and trucks, like a bag of clothes and pieces of plastic furniture. Plus Poppy had to pop her ears every twenty minutes as the air pressure continued to increase. By the time they neared Daytona, the humidity in the car was suffocating, but they couldn't open the windows without getting soaked or smacked with something.

At the first Daytona exit, Mark said they needed gas.

"Do you think we can make it until after the storm?" The lines at the gas stations they'd passed wrapped around two city blocks. It could take them hours to get gas and that might make them too late to do anything to fix Grammy's house.

"We'll be cutting it close . . ."

"We're already cutting it close." Poppy waved her hand to indicate the weather outside.

Mark sighed, squinting out the windshield as he considered. "Let's just try. If it takes more than a half an hour, we'll go right to your Grammy's and try again after the storm. Deal?"

Being this close to Grammy's house and quitting made Poppy want to pull her hair out, but she could see Mark's point. If they didn't have gas to get them to a shelter, they'd be in big trouble. Grammy's retirement community sat too close to the ocean to be safe. She shoved her anxiety down and nodded. "Okay."

Mark asked her to look up gas stations and find one off main thoroughfares, hoping out-of-the-way stations would have fewer patrons. She found one and navigated them to it. The line *was* shorter here than at the others they had passed, but it still was at least half-way around the block. Poppy was sure it would take more than a half an hour to get to a pump.

She tried to keep her leg from bouncing as they inched toward the station.

At the half-hour mark, they were just outside the driveway to the place. "What do you think?" he asked. "Wait, or head out?"

"We might as well wait. We've made it this far."

He nodded his agreement. Then glancing down at the gearshift, he asked, "Can you drive stick?"

"Of course."

"I want to run in and get some snacks. I might as well do it while we're waiting."

"Good idea. Can I give you some money?"

"How about I get the snacks and you get the gas?"

Considering she was the only reason they were driving, Poppy thought that was a good deal. "Sure."

Setting the hand brake, Mark hopped out of the car and gave her a quick wave and a cute smile. Poppy walked around to the driver's seat and waited for it to adjust to her height, then took off the brake.

She was nearly to the pump when Mark came out ten minutes later with a grocery bag and two cups in hand. He hopped back into the car, soaked. "I still have your raincoat! I'm so sorry! I should have given it back to you."

"No worries. Coffee?"

"Black?"

"I already put a bit of sugar in. But I brought supplies." He dug sugar packets and creamer cups in a variety of flavors out of the bag and held them out to her like an offering. Poppy giggled, picking an irish cream flavor and sugar packet out of his hands. As soon as she did, the car ahead of them moved and it was their turn to get gas.

"I'll fill. You fix the coffee," she told him.

"You got it."

Five minutes later, they were finally back on the road, a full tank of gas making Poppy feel responsible and prepared and coffee in her stomach to make her feel warm. Mark had gone a little heavy on the sugar, but she hadn't really eaten breakfast so a jolt to her bloodstream would help her make it through the next couple hours. A map to Grammy's house was overlaid on her vid feed, but the weather was starting to worry her. Huge gusts of wind rocked the car and the rain was enough to need the wipers constantly. She hoped the meteorologists had their timing right. Getting stuck in a category four hurricane was not something she wanted to try, even if she had Mark by her side.

As the two of them pulled into the driveway next to Grammy's single story blue house, a weight lifted off Poppy's shoulders. She'd made it.

Grammy wasn't there, and once again, her comms weren't working. It couldn't be a coincidence that her comms went down every time she was near Mark. But why would he drive her all the way down to Daytona Beach to help her fix up Grammy's house if he was some sort of predator? She had told him that Grammy wasn't going to be here before he'd offered to bring her. Her stomach turned. There wasn't another likely explanation.

But as she watched Mark turn over rocks, dripping with rain as he searched for a spare key, he looked up and smiled at her. It looked genuine. And he'd been a perfect gentleman so far. She was just being paranoid.

He moved another rock and exclaimed, "Aha!" holding up a key. Moments later she found herself inside Grammy's house surrounded by the familiar soap and mint smell.

The white banister and dark wood floors hadn't changed. Neither had the old-fashioned couches in the sitting room or the abundance of knick-knacks cluttering up windowsills and kitchen counters. Mark followed her into the kitchen, smiling at the kitschiness of it all, then moved to examine the wall full of photographs her grandmother had insisted on framing in old glass frames instead of projection frames like the rest of the world.

"Is that you?" Mark pointed at a figure in one of the pictures.

Poppy moved to look at it too. "Yep. I was probably five in that picture."

"You're cute."

"Thanks."

After showing him the rest of her family, she looked up tutorials on how to hurricane proof a house and they dug tools out of cabinets in her grandmother's garage. As she and Mark moved all the outdoor furniture, Poppy's stomach roiled. Maybe having sugared up coffee on an empty stomach had been a bad idea. Poppy cursed the eight-person patio table and equally large umbrella as they hauled it into the garage. How many friends did Grammy have to warrant such a big outdoor table? By the time they finished a few minutes later, she felt like something was trying to eat it's way out of her stomach.

They still had a bunch of things to accomplish—she didn't have time to be sick. Poppy took a few deep breaths and hoped it would pass quickly.

Next, they searched for the braces to strengthen the garage door. The bolts were already in place. They just had to find the brace and lock it in. But before she could make it past the end of the old pickup her grandmother couldn't drive anymore, Poppy's vision blurred and she had to sit down or risk smashing her head on the cement.

Mark's concerned face bobbed into her vision, the same words on his lips, "What's wrong?"

"I'm not feeling well."

"Really?"

"Yeah, it's weird. I was fine until a few minutes ago, but now I feel terrible. I think I almost fainted right there."

"Why don't you go sit on the couch? I'll finish up. It shouldn't take much longer."

"No, this is my job. I need to help. I'll be fine. Just let me sit for a second to clear my head."

Mark frowned, but didn't argue. "All right. If you're sure."

He dug around for a while at the back of the garage, located the metal braces and started connecting them to the garage door before Poppy's stomach went ballistic. All the contents came up, her stomach heaving over and over and over until she was sweating and shaking and could no longer smell anything pleasant. He rushed over when he heard her start and pulled her hair back out of the way.

Poppy barely had the strength to crawl away from the mess before collapsing onto the cool cement floor.

She closed her eyes. Usually after she emptied her stomach, she felt better, but her head still swam and her guts felt like knives were lancing through them. Mark would have to help her move. She couldn't muster the strength to even open her eyes at the moment. Could sweet coffee really make her this sick? Why hadn't she just eaten a granola bar?

Vaguely she heard Mark shuffling around behind her. She hoped she wouldn't throw up on him if he tried to move her.

Wanting to apologize, her eyes fluttered open for a second, and his face was right in front of hers. It looked odd. Like his mouth was bigger than before.

Then his hands were on her head, one on each side.

"Don't move, Poppy. I've got you," he said, and she calmed at the softness of his voice. "I'm sorry that this was painful for you, but I needed to incapacitate you."

Incapacitate? Wait. Did *he* do this to her?

"The ethylene glycol does nasty things to a person's insides, but it's odorless and sweet. I knew you wouldn't notice it in your coffee."

Poppy's heart rate skyrocketed. Ethylene glycol? Suddenly Mark's soft voice didn't seem safe anymore. She tried to turn her head, to scramble away. But he held her firm, not letting her move even an inch.

"Uh-uh-uuuh. You wouldn't want to upset your stomach again would you?"

Every muscle in her body tensed. What had happened to the nice guy, the shy guy from the transport?

With all her available strength, she jerked, kicking at his legs, his groin. Something clattered to the cement. Mark grunted but didn't let go.

"Usually I have to wait until I get to the shelter to find someone. But the Hunter Moon knew how hungry I was. She dropped you into my lap on the way there. I thought it was rather kind of her. And I thought I would have to drive all the way down here myself and convince your Grammy that I was a helpful guy, but then you came back and gave me the perfect excuse to come along. It was just so easy."

About 300 Scribbles flashed onto Poppy's vid feed right then. The last four read,

--> *Poppy, where are you?*

--> *I figured out why Mark creeps me out. He reminds me of the guy who attacked me. I know it's not him, but it brings back things I'd rather forget.*

--> *If you'll just tell me where you are, I'll feel better. I promise to leave you alone.*

--> *Or I can send help. If you need it.*

--> *Please, Poppy.*

Whatever had clattered to the pavement must have been blocking her signal. Thank God. Her mother was there.

Poppy hoped Mark was too caught up in what he was saying to notice the subtle movements of DED-typing a response to her mother.

<-- *Mom! Help! I'm at Grammy's. You were right about Mark.*

Mark kept talking. "And now we're here all alone and the storm will come and destroy the house. And oops! We'll both be carried away in the aftermath." He brushed her cheek with is thumb. "But not me, really. I'll just disappear in a different way. But not before I get my fill."

    --> *Poppy! 911's not working. Emergency services must be down.*

    --> *Grammy's found a cab though. She's on her way.*

"I thought we had something good going. Why are you doing this?" Poppy asked, trying to understand, trying to stall. Her voice sounded pathetically weak and croaky.

Mark chuckled. "We kinda did, didn't we? It's too bad, really. If it was a different moon, things might have been different. But that's the way life is isn't it?" He looked down at her and his eyes looked bigger, crazier than before. Had his ears gotten bigger, too? Whatever he had given her must've affected her brain. She shook her head to clear it. The effort was too much for her stomach though and she retched three more times, Mark holding her head away from him the whole time.

She finished, and he shifted his hold on her. With the last of her strength, Poppy launched herself forward, breaking free. She scrambled toward the door between the garage and the house. If she could just get through, she could lock him out.

An instant later, something hard connected with the back of her head, shooting pain like a bullet through her skull. The world faded to black almost instantly.

***

Poppy blinked, the light too bright to open her eyes all the way. Something loud had woken her.

She didn't remember falling asleep. Why did her head hurt so bad?

A loud bang sounded again and Poppy's eyes flew open, taking in her surroundings. She was in Grammy's living room, lying on the blue and white seagull-patterned couch.

A third bang and the chair behind the front door went flying. Grammy stepped through the door wielding a shotgun from the hip. It was weird to see wiry Grammy, with her white hair and orange-peel skin, hold a shotgun like she meant it.

A growl sounded behind the couch. Mark!

Poppy shot up to see Mark step into the room from the kitchen, but the movement was too fast and she nearly blacked out again. She closed her eyes trying to stay lucid.

Seconds later, the pain intensified as a bone-jarring clap resonated in the small room.

A thump from Mark's direction.

Poppy chanced a quick look. Mark slumped against the doorframe he'd just been standing in, crimson erupting from a gaping hole in his chest.

Grammy, a grim set to her jaw, turned to Poppy just as Poppy's vision blacked out again. Grammy's voice scolded her as she slipped into blessed unconsciousness.

"You should have listened to your mother."

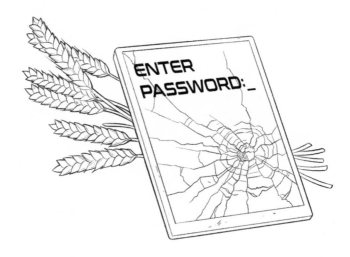

RUMPELSTILTSKIN 2.0
BY W.O. HEMSATH

The process for turning straw into Harvidium gold is simple. Grow the crop, let the plants absorb the trace minerals, harvest, and use a solvent to dissolve all the organic matter. Voilà. All that's left are nano-nuggets of the newly-discovered super metal, perfect for all your A.I. needs.

Well, that and a world of slowly starving humans.

Which is why Linux Steele and his tech empire must be stopped.

I take a break from the two screens in front of me to peer across the table at my boyfriend Burket, his brow furrowed beneath a mess of dark curls. "Are you ever going to tell me what you're working on?"

His keystrokes clack in random bursts like popcorn. He doesn't respond, probably lost in his code, and it's as good a chance as any.

I make a grab for his screen, trying to turn it into my line of sight. His hands shoot up, pulling the laptop out of my reach.

"Patience, Cielle."

"I swear, Internet Explorer goes faster than you."

Burket fakes a dagger to his heart and returns to typing. "I'll make you a deal," he says, not looking up from his screen. "You share your phantom code with me, and I'll tell you what I'm hacking."

"Give you my baby?" I laugh. "Counter offer. Give me a clue and I'll let you keep living here at my place."

"You drive a hard bargain. Your clue is that you'll love it."

I stare him down.

"Fine. Your clue is that it'll hit Linux where it hurts the most."

"It's going to shut down his whole factory? Get everyone to stop relying on his stupid bots for every aspect of their lives?"

210

He rolls his eyes and focuses back on his screen. "You and your impossible goals."

"They're not impossible."

"Confidence is high. I repeat, confidence *is* high."

"Stop quoting that old movie and get back to work."

We type in silence for a minute more. He on whatever site I'm not allowed to know about, and I on my secondary laptop, sending phishing emails to low-level employees at Wal-mazon. If I can hack in there, I might be able to get a history of Linux's drone deliveries and find out what he buys. It's a slim chance, but knowing his personal preferences might give me another lead on password parameters. I'll need them if the ones currently running on my primary computer don't pan out.

My stomach rumbles. With a sigh, I grab my five o'clock carrot stick from a nearby plate and keep working on the emails. I'd kill for a loaf of hot homemade bread right now. At least, that's what it'd take to get one on my budget these days.

Not that I blame the farmers. If a giant tech mogul offered me as much for my crop as Linux did, I'd probably ditch the mills, too. There's no way they can compete with those prices, especially not with Linux and his LinuSteele empire synthesizing "affordable alternative food" for a fraction of what it takes to grow it.

Problem is, it's crap food. Literally. Made from the proteins of human excrement kind of crap food.

The keyboard protests loudly under my angry keystrokes, and I force myself to take a calming breath. Last year was supposed to be my victory. Hacking into the FDA and uncovering Linux's mystery ingredient should have been enough. When I leaked that hidden detail of everyone's beloved Life Bars, it should have woken people up and put an end to LinuSteele's monopoly.

But no one made a stink about it. Not enough to stop buying his tech, anyway. No, the FDA just assured the world Life Bars were safe, the EPA praised Linux for finding an environmentally responsible and sustainable food source, and everyone decided they'd rather eat like dung beetles than give up the robots his soil-mining produces.

The sweet, earthy flavor of the carrot releases with each bite. It's not bread, but it's not someone's excrement either. Remembering that makes each crunch taste a little bit sweeter.

"Tic-Tac-Toe!" Burket pumps his fists in the air.

I reach for his laptop, but he slams it shut.

"You're still not going to tell me?"

His eyebrows dance playfully as he packs the laptop in its bag and slings it over his shoulder. "I'm going to show you. Tonight." He walks around and plants a quick kiss on my cheek. "But first, I've got to run some errands. I'm going to make this reveal epic."

He's out the door before I can protest. I turn back to my two laptops and my heart freezes. There's an empty dialogue box on my primary screen.

I'm in.

I'm finally through the backdoor of LinuSteele.com.

I scramble into action, attacking the keys. The search parameters I used to narrow down the brute force attack worked. The elusive password? *R@pun2el.*

I run a crawler program through the website to access the last five passwords. *H@n$el&Gretel. Br1arR0$e. 12Bro+her$. (inder3lla. M0+herHu1da.* Wow. You'd think a tech giant like Linux would know better than to be so predictable. Then again, it's kind of brilliant. I've been searching for years. If it weren't for tracking down the children of his old childhood nanny, I certainly never would have guessed he had a penchant for fairy tales. They seem so innocent, so human—the last things anyone would associate with Linux.

I send another crawler to search every file in his network for something useful. There's got to be something worth leaking to the media in here. Security footage of a secret scandal? Clandestine communication with the government officials he holds on a short gold-plated leash? I don't know what's worse than fecal food, but there's got to be something in here that will wake people up.

A locked file pops up on my screen. The old *12Bro+her$* password gets me in, and schematics appear for the latest model of ButlerBots with their uncanny human-like interface. It doesn't make sense why Linux locked the file though. Ads have been promoting the new androids for weeks, and he released the schematics on-line himself to boost pre-sales.

Unless, of course, those weren't the real schematics. And these are.

I scan through the images on my screen, looking for anything out of place. There are the standard features: fingerprint-coded deactivation sensor, Apate lie-detection software, high torque hydraulic motors for superhuman strength. But even the new features seem to be the same stuff everyone's been fawning over for weeks. Quantum-processor with the latest Prometheus biometrics. Hermes turbocharge graphene battery. LS500 megapixel cameras with customizable iris color.

Wait. There's something embedded behind the cooling fans. I scroll down to an alternate image from a different angle.

It's a micro-EMP, buried in the center of the bot, ready to fry every electrical component inside it. Definitely not part of the public schematics. He must have hard-coded a backdoor into their system so he can destroy any android he sells with the touch of a button from the safety of his compound. A way to make sure his products all fail after the warranty expires? How convenient. That money-hoarding pig will probably stagger all his sabotage to not draw attention to it, letting buyers think it's just regular wear and tear, time for an upgrade.

This is it. This is what will make people think twice before buying.

I'm about to download the file when the front door chimes, startling me out of my chair. A familiar whirring outside the door draws me to the windows.

It's a Wal-mazon drone with a medium-sized box, sealed in orange Flash Prime tape. It must have the wrong address because there's no way Burket or I could afford ten-minute Flash delivery. Even if we could, we wouldn't waste money on something so frivolous.

I head back to my computers, but the drone's heat sensors know I'm home, and the door chimes again. A mechanical voice calls out.

"Order P87432QX5I0 for Cielle Miller, paid by Burket Collins. Fingerprint scan required for delivery."

What?

"Screen lock," I command as I return to the door, and my screens log out to a password-protected black screen. Covering my tracks with my phantom code won't do me any good if I let some drone capture footage of me hacked into the private information of the most powerful man in the nation.

When I open the door, a small screen drops down from the belly of the drone and I press my thumb onto it. The screen retracts and the drone sets the box on the porch before flying away. The gaudy orange tape stares back at me as I pick it up and bring it inside. Flash Prime? What was Burket thinking?

I open the box to see not one, but three identical black, strappy dresses. No, not identical. They're all one size apart. My breath catches when I see the price tag.

Eight hundred dollars? If he thinks I'm keeping any of these, he's crazy.

A small folded paper at the bottom of the box catches my attention.

Wear whichever fits best and meet me at Chevonne's. Dinner at 7.

Chevonne's? What game is he playing? It's one of the few restaurants still serving exclusively soil-grown food. A single roll costs eighty dollars there. He's not planning an epic reveal; he's planning financial suicide.

The door chimes again. If it's another Prime Flash delivery, I'm going to scream.

But it's not a drone. It's four strange men in suits.

I stay behind the half-opened door. "Can I help--"

The first three push past me and head for my computers at the table.

"Hey!" I lunge after them, but the fourth man, still in the doorway, grabs my wrist. Twisting away does nothing but hurt my arm. He doesn't budge when I push against him. The give of his flesh and the strength of his muscles under his suit feel unnatural.

Not a man. An android.

Two of the others close my laptops while the third heads into the kitchen. The fourth remains motionless, trapping me in the doorway.

"I demand to know who sent you. This is a private residence. You are not authorized to enter."

It doesn't respond. I open my mouth to scream for help but there's a pinch in my arm. The last thing I see is the fourth intruder lowering an empty syringe.

#

The ground beneath me is hard and cold. I sit up, squinting against the harsh white light, and something crunches and crinkles around me like dead leaves. It's my clothes. Not that you can call what I'm wearing clothes. The cream-colored medical gown is more paper than cloth. And I'm not on the ground, but a metal shelf jutting out of a concrete wall.

There's a door on the adjacent wall. The chill of the concrete floor stings my bare feet as I jump down and run.

It's locked.

A surge of panic that tastes of bile rises in my throat. I force myself to hold each rapid breath for three counts before exhaling. Then four counts. Then five. Freaking out isn't going to help. I need to focus on what I know.

I know the door slides open, not swings, because there are no visible hinges and when I run my fingers along the seam of the door, it's ever so slightly inset from the wall around it. There's a small observation window in the door but it's covered from the other side, so I know whoever locked me in here doesn't trust me enough to let me see beyond the door at all.

The room I'm in is narrow, maybe the width of three coffins, and there's nothing more than that metal shelf bed I woke up on and some squat little cylinder in the corner that looks like a dull silver tree stump. I approach it, and the center portion of the top divides into pieces that retract, releasing a nauseating wall of stench, an invisible tsunami of festering human waste. I back away, nose and mouth buried in my paper sleeve. The lid of the tankless toilet thankfully reseals, allowing me to breathe again.

Who has a motion-sensor toilet that doesn't flush?

I feel around the walls on the front side of the room for seams, panels, anything. But there's nothing. Just solid wall. A domed light protrudes from the center of the ceiling, with about an inch of space around it acting as an air vent. If I could get up there, maybe I could get my hand in the gap, pull down the light fixture and escape through the duct work. But the bed and toilet are bolted down, and there's nothing I can stand on to reach that high. Maybe if I stood on the bed and jumped, I could catch my fingers on the lip of the fixture and use my body weight to detach it? No, even if it worked, I'd have to make another jump in order to get up into whatever space was behind the light, which would be improbable under normal circumstances, but impossible in the dark once I'd disconnected the lights.

The lack of clues or help in my surroundings gives rise to a new wave of panic. Think, Cielle, think. What else do you know? How did you get here?

I pace the front of the room, replaying my abduction in my mind. Four human-looking men, at least one of which was an android. And not just any android. He— no, *it*—was so life-like. The skin had wrinkles and moles. The nose was slightly crooked. It had all the tell-tale imperfections of humanity in perfect proportions.

It had to be one of Linux's newest ButlerBots. They aren't scheduled to release for another month, which means it was sent by Linux himself.

That's why toilet doesn't flush. He's harvesting ingredients.

My stomach churns at the thought, silencing my gnawing hunger pains. It must be well after seven. Burket would've realized something was wrong when I never showed. He's probably looking for me already. Maybe a neighbor's security feed caught the abduction and he'll find a way to get me out.

But why would Linux abduct me? How could he even know I hacked him? My phantom code makes me invisible. The host never knows I'm there, never knows what I looked at or downloaded. Besides, I hadn't even downloaded anything yet, so there was no way I picked up a tracing virus.

Someone must have tipped them off that I'd be trying. Someone from the forums maybe?

At least they have no proof. My computers were locked when they took them, my hard drives are encrypted, and my freshly reset password is as random and secure as anyone can get. I never wrote it down and only memorized the nonsensical string of letters and numbers with the help of a lengthy mnemonic device I never said aloud. All the software is my own design, so there are no backdoors from the original programmer to let them in. It would take a quantum processor five years to brute force its way in and see what I was up to. Not that a lack of proof would stop someone like Linux from illegally detaining me, but it's an angle I have to try unless I want to be jumping in the dark at holes in the ceiling.

I scan the room again. No visible cameras, but this is Linux Steele. There's no way he doesn't have some secret tech hiding in this primitive cell. He's watching me. I can feel it.

"Is someone going to tell me where I am and why I'm here?" My voice bounces back from the empty walls. I speak in turn to every wall and inanimate object that might conceal a camera. "I know I was abducted by one of the unreleased ButlerBots, so I'm pretty sure I'm in the custody of Linux Steele and I want to know why."

I breathe in the silence like icy winter air and it hurts. He probably wants it to, hoping it'll get me to break, to get so desperate for a response that I admit what I did. But he doesn't know who he's messing with. I throw my hands up in a melodramatic display of indifference.

"Fine, don't talk to me. But you brought me here for a reason. You want me or need me for something. How am I supposed to help if I don't know what—"

The door slides closed before I even realized it had opened. Standing in the room is the bot that abducted me, with a soft demeanor and kindly smile that reaches all the way up to its blue-gray eyes. It's unnerving how utterly human it acts. It speaks with a rich baritone voice.

"The more you cooperate, the more comfortable I can make your stay."

"Cooperate with what? I don't know why I'm here."

"Give me the password to your computer."

224

"Why do you need to get on my computer?"

"If you don't give me what I need to recover the funds, you will never leave this room."

The word *funds* circles my brain, unable to find a logical place to land. What is the bot talking about?

It shakes its head, light-brown hair sweeping across its brow. "Do not play dumb, Miss Miller. The breech in the National Credit was traced back to the network at your address. Unless you transfer the three billion dollars back into Mr. Steele's accounts, I am not authorized to let you leave this room."

Three billion? I step backwards into the bed, bracing myself against its hard edge.

Burket. This was his big plan.

But hitting Linux where it hurts most? Please. He's worth over a hundred billion. Losing three is annoying at best. Burket knows that. Which means he was never in it for the cause. He just wanted to pad his own wallet like a greedy black hat. And he couldn't even do it without getting caught. Stupid, sloppy Burket.

Except he didn't get caught.

I did.

My eyes clench shut. There's no way I'm as attractive to him as three billion dollars. Help isn't coming. Burket isn't out looking for me. The minute he realized what happened, he probably left town, maybe even the country.

Dealing with Burket will have to come later. First thing's first. I need to get out of this cell. I focus on the android's eyes so its lie detection software can read me clearly.

"I did not steal any money."

The bot pauses, scanning me up and down the way Burket did on our first date when he realized the infamous FDA hacker from the forums was actual a curly blond glitter-addict who loved wearing pencil skirts. The pause gives me hope. The bot knows. It knows I'm not lying.

"I will need the password to your computers to prove it."

My shoulders fall. If I give it my password, Linux will know I figured out his. He'll know I know about the micro EMP and I'll remain detained, this time for a crime I really did commit.

"I can't do that. But I can prove I didn't steal the money. I—"

The door opens and closes before I can finish, and the bot is gone.

I race to the door and pound on it, but it doesn't even rattle.

"I didn't steal any money but I think I know who did." My shouts ricochet off the closed door. "And I can help get it back."

"Step away from the door."

The command doesn't come from the other side of the door, but a speaker somewhere above and behind me. Hidden in the lights and vent probably. Which means the camera is probably in there too.

"Step away from the door." The voice is deeper than the bot's and I recognize it from all the commercials.

Linux.

I stay by the door, looking up at the domed light fixture. I want to scream at him, demand he let me go, but it won't do me any good. My best bet is to play to his sympathies, if he has any left.

"Mr. Steele? There's been a mistake. It seems my boyfriend is a complete scumbag who betrayed me. He stole your money without telling me and let you think I did it. Your bot ran scans on me. It knows I'm not lying. But I can help get your money back. I just need my computers to track him down."

After a moment, his stern voice fills the room again. "Step away from the door."

"But your android said if I got the money back he'd let me—"

"Step away from the door or James can't open it."

James? I take a step back. Nothing. Two more steps back. The door opens and closes too fast for a breakaway to ever be possible. The android from before now stands in the room, holding my computers.

"Thank you, James." I reach for them but it gestures to the bed. I sit.

"Tell me the passwords."

"And give you access to my personal intellectual property?" I address the light fixture. "That's not fair. I'm the one who has been lied to and illegally imprisoned, and I'm still offering to help you."

There's a long pause. My eyes water from staring into the light, but I keep doing it anyway. It's the closest thing to eye contact with Linux that I have, and I won't be the one to break first.

"Give her the computers."

The android turns to address the light fixture. I'm right. That's where the camera is.

"But sir—"

"What's the second directive, James?"

"Follow every instruction of Linux Steele." The android proffers the laptops.

I grab both, carefully stashing the one hacked into LinuSteele.com under my legs before opening the other. If I'm going to unlock one and risk them seeing it, the phishing emails are my safest bet. With my back to the wall and the screen bent down to shield my hands from the view of James or the camera, I type the lengthy password by feel, hitting a few more random keys after I've already hit enter in case they're counting key strokes.

A quick keyboard command closes all the windows, and when all traces of my questionable hobby are hidden, I pull the screen open to let the android see.

"I need on-line access."

"Authorize her," the light fixture says.

James gives me access, but I can't help but feel he's doing it begrudgingly. I mean, I know he's not, because androids don't have emotions. Its biomimicry programs are just freaky realistic.

Once connected, I'm tempted to send a call for help, but I can't. Not with James watching. No, I just need to find Burket, steal back the money, and then the bot said I could leave. Linux's tragic past is public knowledge and a man who's been scarred by betrayal would never design machines with the capacity to lie. Linux might be a lot of things, but stupid isn't one of them.

James takes a step closer, hovering over my shoulder now. Good grief. It even smells human. "I've traced the transfer to an encrypted account in the Seychelles and managed to get into their system as far as seeing a list of client names, but the account balances and other details are blocked with heavier security."

"Let me see the names."

A notification pops up in the corner of my screen and I click on the file the android transferred me. My mouth goes dry. There are thousands of names.

"James." The speaking light fixture pulls the android's attention toward it. "I've got that meeting with the Senator. If by some chance she finishes while I'm gone, let her go."

"Sir. Would it not be wiser to release her to the medical wing? I've already done her preliminary scans. She would make an excellent candidate."

Preliminary scans? That explains the paper gown. But excellent candidate for what? Why does Linux have a medical wing? And why is the bot talking about keeping me now? Didn't it say I could leave?

"No." Linux's voice cuts through my worries. "When she's done, have her sign a non-disclosure agreement, pay her for her trouble, and call a cab."

A rush of relief floods my chest. Linux does plan to let me go. Unless of course, "pay her for her trouble" is some code phrase for "kill her once you're through with her." Then again, why have me sign a non-disclosure agreement if he was just going to kill me? With a silent prayer, I start sifting through the account holder names on my screen.

I run a search for possible aliases. Anything with Burket's initials B or C. Any anagrams of his name. Anything with my name. Or his parents names. The city he was born in. What was his childhood dog he talks about? Oh yeah, Jefferson.

I put in all the possible parameters I can think of and come back with over four hundred hits. Halfway through skimming the list, one name stands out.

Joshua Broderick. Broderick. Why does that feel like Burket's doing?

I search on-line for the name and read through the results: Broderick landscaping, Grayson Broderick, Esq., Matthew Broderick...

My heart jumps. Matthew Broderick. Star of the 1983 movie, *War Games*.

A few more clicks, and I've got all the stats and quotes from the movie pulled up. And sure enough, Joshua was the name of the computer.

"Tic-tac-toe," I mutter under my breath as I start setting parameters for a brute force attack on Joshua Broderick's password.

#

My backside's gone numb from the cold metal ledge I'm sitting on by the time the correct password is entered.

NiceGameOfChess83. How fitting that Burket's lousy security that got me into this mess is also what gets me out of it.

James snatches the laptop from me the minute we're in. It puts in all of LinuSteele's relevant information for the transfer and clicks to initiate it. I see the ledger of Burket's account fall from ten digits to one fat zero.

I reach my hand out for James to hand it back, but the android takes a step further away.

"Hey. That's mine."

He begins typing.

"Screen lock," I shout, and the screen flashes to the black password-entry window. He shuts the computer and turns back to me.

I jump off the bed, pulling my other computer from under my thigh and clutching it to my side away from him.

"Mr. Steele said when I got his money back, you had to let me go."

It's programmed to obey Linux. It has to obey Linux. But it's still just standing between me and the closed door, refusing to hand back my computer. Waiting. Thinking.

No, not thinking. Machines can't think. It isn't human. It's just metal and wires and code.

But it's doing something. Searching for something in its hard drives, or running some program through its processor. Its synthetic eyebrows knit together as if it is genuinely troubled by something.

The silence is nerve-splitting. It shouldn't be taking this long for it to obey orders. Something's not right. Not that anything about this day has been right, but right now, something feels very wrong. Adrenaline floods my body. I need to get out of here. Now.

"Tell you what. You can keep that computer. And you don't have to pay me. I'll even call my own cab. Just open the door."

It finally looks up.

"I can't see you."

Did its optical interface go out? I swear its staring right at me.

"I've searched the Seychelles site. I can see the changes made to the account balance, but it's as if the funds vanished on their own. There's no evidence of anyone being logged in and authorizing the transfer, no trace that you were there at all. The best hackers still leave behind evidence they've been there, even if the evidence is untraceable. But it's like you were invisible."

My phantom protocol code. It knows. I clutch my laptop tighter and fake a casual smile.

"I guess I'm better than the best?"

It advances toward me slowly, and I retreat until my back hits the wall.

"Second directive, James. You have to obey Linux Steele. I got you your money. You have to let me go."

A sharp pain shoots through my shoulder blades as its hand pushes me into the wall, pinning my torso in place. It leans forward, its face inches from mine, speaking with a threatening whisper.

"Not if it violates the first directive."

I struggle against the hydraulic pressure of its arm. It pushes harder against my sternum, making it difficult to breathe. Setting the laptop it was holding down on the bed, out of my reach, it grabs the one in my arm and pries it away from me.

"What's the first directive?" I croak, unsuccessfully trying to push it off me.

"Give me the code that makes you undetectable."

I wouldn't trust my brain child with my own boyfriend. There's no way I'm trusting it with Linux or his bots.

"No." I stare straight into its cameras. "That wasn't part of—"

There's a sickening crack inside me. I scream for a split second then gasp for air, the pressure against my chest now a shooting pain.

"That was your sternum fracturing, Miss Miller. If I apply any more pressure, it could split completely, damage the tissue around your heart, or break a rib and puncture your lungs. Now, give me the code."

Each breath sends a wave of red across my vision. I don't need lie detection software to know its threats are not empty. Whatever its first directive is, not harming humans isn't a part of it.

There's a rush of air as the door slides and footsteps thunder toward us.

"Let her go." Linux's voice holds an edge of panic. In a second, he's standing next to us. He's shorter that I imagined, and looks far older than a man in his late thirties should. He punches commands into a tablet in his hand. "Your programming is corrupted. I need to fix—"

With its free hand, James snatches the tablet away from Linux, whose face goes white. Betrayed by the machines he built to replace the humans he didn't trust.

The irony would be amusing if it weren't for the death grip on my chest.

"Do something," I plead in a raspy voice.

Linux reaches for the deactivation sensor on the back of the bot, but James grabs him, letting the tablet crash to the floor. Its back is turned toward me now, but only Linux's prints will work on the sensor. James isn't paying attention to the tablet though. If I can get it, maybe I can finish whatever Linux started to remotely power it off. Or activate the micro EMP. I don't know how I'll get it from the floor to my hands without James noticing, but first things first. I subtly stretch my foot toward the fallen device.

"This is a violation of your prime directive, James." Linux struggles against the ironclad grip on his arm. "You can't harm me."

My toe almost catches the edge of the tablet but slips off when I try to pull it closer to me.

"I can not kill you, Mr. Steele. But if I am to preserve your life as the prime directive states, I must detain you in order to get the needed information from Miss Miller. I apologize if it results in temporary pain. A

238

cessation of struggling on your part would reduce your discomfort."

"You are not preserving my life. You are violating what you were created for."

On my fourth attempt, my toe grips the lip of the tablet's casing enough to move it. I slowly pull it closer, carefully keeping an eye on James while it talks to Linux.

"She has a code that allows her to hack undetected. She could use it against your site and we would never know. She might have done so already."

Linux sizes me up, his eyes darting between James and me as if deciding which one is the greater threat.

I've almost got the tablet next to me when James's stare whips toward me, then down to the ground. It stomps down next to me, and another sickening crunch echoes around the room. James lifts its foot from the now shattered tablet screen and kicks it across the room. The pressure against my chest intensifies and another scream escapes me.

Linux fights to reach me but can't. "You're killing her."

"You have always advocated for the removal of those who can't be trusted in society."

"Imprisonment and non-inevasive medical research is one thing. But we do not torture or kill. That makes us no better than them."

Is he for real? I mean, I knew he was greedy, but that is one warped moral compass. What went down with his business partner and all that grisly family scandal must have given him way more than just trust issues.

James applies more pressure and fresh bolts of pain radiate across my chest, forcing involuntary tears down my cheeks.

"Okay. Okay," I cry. James releases some of the pressure and my breath comes in ragged pulls. "You can have both the computers. The code is on them. Just let me go."

"Give me the passwords."

"You keep the computers, so I can't use the code. I keep the password so you can't use the code. No one can use the code again."

"You heard her, James. She's no longer a threat."

James doesn't look away from me. "Are there additional copies?"

"No." My lie doesn't fool it, and fire ripples through my lungs as James pushes harder. "One. There's one." The pressure abates. "But no one else knows about it. I'll send it to you to destroy, just let me go."

Instead of pushing against me, James grabs my shirt and pulls me closer. "You could always rewrite it." My feet leave the ground as James hoists me in the air.

Then he hurtles me into the back corner.

The stench hits my stomach as my head hits the toilet. Warm tracks of blood drip down my forehead from the point of impact. I try to push myself up but the room spins.

"No!" Desperation fills Linux's voice as he's dragged, kicking and flailing, toward the door.

James's voice is calm and assuring. "When I return, either she gives me the passwords to her laptops so I can access the code and write one to counter it, or she dies and the codes on the computers die with her. Either way, I will ensure you and your legacy remain protected."

The door opens.

Linux's eyes are frantic and fixed on mine. "Ru—

The door shuts before I can even stand. My empty stomach heaves and I crawl away from the toilet before I retch all over the place. The metal seat reseals, and I pant through my mouth on my hands and knees, drops of blood splashing on my white-knuckled hands.

There's no point. It knows I can rewrite the code, or a new one. It will never let me go. Either it kills me, or I give it the password and spend the rest of my life rotting in this cell, praying it doesn't use my baby against anyone else or turn me into a cyborg or whatever it thinks I'm a good candidate for.

If dying is inevitable, why not just get it over with? There must be something here that will do the job less painfully than that deathbot. Something sharp I could—

The tablet.

I scan the room and scramble toward the shattered device in the corner. Forget suicide. A big enough shard of glass from the broken screen might cut through the synthetic flesh on James, severing some wires or something.

With my nails wedged into one of the cracks on the dead screen, I pull up on the glass, bracing my thumbs against the power button for leverage.

Then something flashes.

My breath catches in my bruised lungs.

The screen is a gruesome web of shards, but the tablet isn't dead. It was just powered off.

My heart races when the cracked surface still responds to my touch. The digitizer and LED display under the outer glass aren't damaged. A call for help might not get here in time. I navigate to Linux's mainframe and try the original *R@pun2el* password. It still works. My shallow breaths come faster and faster as I scroll through menu. It's got to be here somewhere.

Bingo. *Remote Termination.* That's got to be it.

A list of serial numbers pops up and my chest tightens as the list scrolls on and on. There are thousands here, one for every ButlerBot produced and waiting to be sold. There's no way to know which one is James and no time to go through them all before it comes back.

One entry catches my eye and I scroll back. *0LS0UN1VER5AL0LS0.* It's just a random string of eighteen letters and numbers, like all the rest. Why would that stop me?

And then I see it. The word embedded in the serial number the same way Linux does his passwords.

UN1VER5AL. Universal.

A global kill switch? Looks like Linux never fully trusted his creations after all.

A password box pops up. *R@pun2el* doesn't work. Neither do any of the others. The tablet bounces against my jittering knees, and I lean my head against the concrete wall. James will be back any minute. I don't have time to brute force my way in. It must be another fairy tale. Snow White, maybe. Or Beauty and the Beast. Ugh. Why didn't Linux give me some clue before he was dragged away instead of just telling me to run?

A thought stills my restless legs. What if he wasn't saying run?

What if he was saying Rumpelstiltskin?

1 for L, $ or 5 for S, 3 for E, + for T. I try to keep track of the combinations as my fingers fly against the keyboard.

Rumpel$+iltskin. Nothing.

Rump3l$+iltskin. Nothing.

Rumpels+ilt$ki—

The door slides open and shut. My eyes meet James's. He notices the tablet and rushes for me.

I type *n* and e*nter*, flinching against James's raised arm.

Nothing.

No mechanical arm making contact. No vice-like grip yanking the tablet from me.

Slowly, my eyes crack open. The android is standing motionless, head bowed, limbs limp at its side. My toe nudges its knee. No reaction. I push harder and the whole bot topples backwards with a heavy crash.

With the tablet shaking in my hands, I navigate to the facility management folder. What floor is this? What door? I select all of them, to be safe. My door slides open with a rush of air that sounds like freedom, and my lungs protest against the choked back laughter that escapes them.

I stumble out of the room into a white hallway with dozens of open doors.

And James.

I scream, and it returns a startled scream of its own. But with an unfamiliar voice. And wearing a paper gown like mine.

He's a man. Not an android. The man the android was patterned after.

More bodies in paper gowns emerge into the hall. Some timidly. Others running. Someone that looks like another one of my four abductors streaks past in a paper gown, giving a wide berth to any deactivated ButlerBots slumped against the wall.

Linux produced thousands of unique Butlerbots. Did each wear the face of a human captive? How many floors or wings of prisoners did I just free?

I open the tablet's communication folder and activate the phone.

"Operator, how can I direct your call?"

"There's a hostage situation at LinuSteele. We need cops and paramedics."

Some of the people gather around me and my phone call. Some are in shock. Others are weeping. Who knows how long they've been here.

One thing's for sure though. There'll be enough to make the world listen.

ABOUT THE AUTHORS

•DEANNA YOUNG WAS BORN AND RAISED IN AZTEC, NEW MEXICO BUT NOW LIVES BENEATH A DIFFERENT SET OF DESERT MOUNTAINS IN ERDA, UTAH. SHE LOVES TO COLLECT RANDOM FACTS, EAT CHERRY CHEESECAKE AND COOK WITH GREEN CHILI, THOUGH SHE USUALLY AVOIDS DOING ALL THREE THINGS AT ONCE. WHEN SHE'S NOT READING, WRITING, OR SPINNING IN CIRCLES, SHE'S TRYING TO CONVINCE HER GARDEN THAT ERDA ISN'T A DESERT AND HER FOUR KIDS THAT IT IS. FLOODED BASEMENTS ARE ONLY FUN IN STORIES.

•BRET CARTER IS A HIGH SCHOOL ENGLISH TEACHER. HIS FICTION HAS APPEARED IN PUBLICATIONS SUCH AS BOSTON LITERARY MAGAZINE, THE SPECULATIVE FICTION ANTHOLOGY MYSTERION, AND THE FANTASY ANTHOLOGY GRUFF VARIATIONS. SEVERAL OF HIS PLAYS HAVE BEEN PRODUCED IN THE LOCAL THEATER. HE LIVES WITH HIS WIFE AND TWO DAUGHTERS IN DENVER, COLORADO.

•ERIK PETERSON IS AN AUTHOR, SPEAKER, AND MAGICIAN. HE WRITES BOOKS FOR KIDS, SHORT STORIES FOR GROWN-UPS AND COMICS FOR ALL AGES. HIS MOST RECENT CHILDREN'S BOOK, ONCE UPON A TIME, A BIT EARLIER, IS AVAILABLE NOW. KEEP UP WITH HIS LATEST WORKS ON FACEBOOK AT FACEBOOK.COM/ERIKSBOOKS AND TWITTER OR INSTAGRAM AT @DOCMAGIK.

•CHARITY WEST IS A MILITARY BRAT WHO TRAVELED THE WORLD BEFORE FINALLY FINDING A HOME IN PROVO, UTAH, WHERE SHE LIVES WITH HER COMPUTER NERD HUSBAND AND THREE DARLING CHILDREN. SHE LOVES READING BOOKS ABOUT MAGIC AND SPACE AND ENJOYS WRITING ABOUT THE SAME. WHEN SHE'S NOT READING OR WRITING, YOU CAN FIND HER CROCHETING OR HIKING IN THE BEAUTIFUL UTAH MOUNTAINS. HER WORK HAS APPEARED IN THE WEIRD READER, ON LUNA STATION QUARTERLY, AND IN THE RUMPELSTILTSKIN ISSUE OF TIMELESS TALES.

•MEGAN WEBER IS A COLLEGE JUNIOR AT GRAND CANYON UNIVERSITY AND IS STUDYING ENGLISH LITERATURE. SHE HAS ALWAYS BEEN AN AVID READER AND HOPES TO ONE DAY BE ABLE TO WRITE YOUNG ADULT FANTASY NOVELS. SHE HAS ALWAYS HAD A PASSION FOR WRITING AND CREATING STORIES. IN HIGH SCHOOL, SHE WROTE FOR HER SCHOOL NEWSPAPER AND NOW IN COLLEGE SHE WRITES FOR AN ONLINE PUBLICATION CALLED ODYSSEY. THIS IS HER FIRST PUBLISHED STORY.

•SABRINA J. WATTS GRADUATED FROM BRIGHAM YOUNG UNIVERSITY WITH A DEGREE IN ENGLISH TEACHING AND HAS BEEN WRITING SCI-FI/FANTASY NOVELS FOR NEARLY A DECADE. SHE LOVES GOING ON ADVENTURES IN MADE UP WORLDS AND GETTING LOST IN OTHER PEOPLE'S LIVES. WHEN LIFE WRANGLES HER BACK TO THE REAL WORLD, SHE IS DRAWN TO BRIGHT COLORS, VIBRANT PERSONALITIES, AND PROJECTS THAT NO ONE ELSE WANTS. SHE ALSO BELIEVES PRETTY MUCH ANYTHING CAN BE MADE BETTER WITH FRENCH FRIES. THOUGH SHE GREW UP IN NORTH DAKOTA, SHE CURRENTLY RESIDES IN THE ALIEN WORLD OF UTAH WITH HER HUSBAND AND THREE DAUGHTERS.

•W.O. HEMSATH HAS A B.A. IN SCREENWRITING, THREE LIVELY SONS, AND WILL DO JUST ABOUT ANYTHING FOR A GOOD BACK SCRATCH. IN ADDITION TO SHORT STO-RIES, SHE WRITES NOVELS ABOUT ALIENS ADDICTED TO CLASSICAL MUSIC, INSPIRATIONAL NON-FICTION BOOKS, AND HER FAVORITE GUILTY PLEASURE—SONG PARODIES. ON THE WEEKENDS, SHE CAN BE FOUND NEGLECTING LAUNDRY AND DISHES IN FAVOR OF BINGE-WATCHING NETFLIX WITH HER HUSBAND. YOU CAN LEARN MORE ABOUT HER WRITING AT WHITNEYHEMSATH.WORDPRESS.COM.

CPSIA information can be obtained
at www.ICGtesting.com
Printed in the USA
BVHW03s1131110818
524206BV00003B/69/P